Busha's Mistress
or Catherine The Fugitive

Cyrus Francis Perkins (1813–67)
Source: Lily Perkins Collection, Jamaica Archives

Busha's Mistress
or Catherine The Fugitive

A Stirring Romance of the Days of Slavery in Jamaica

Cyrus Francis Perkins
(1813–67)

Edited & Introduced by
Paul E. Lovejoy, Verene A. Shepherd & David V. Trotman

Ian Randle Publishers
Kingston • Miami

First published in Jamaica, 2003 by
Ian Randle Publishers
11 Cunningham Avenue
Box 686, Kingston 6
www.ianrandlepublishers.com

Reprinted with minor revisions 2005

National Library of Jamaica Cataloguing in Publication Data

Perkins, Cyrus Francis
     Busha's mistress or Catherine the fugitive : a stirring romance of the days of slavery / Cyrus Francis Perkins ; edited and introduced by Paul E. Lovejoy, Verene A. Shepherd and David V. Trotman

          p. ; cm

ISBN 976-637-044-3

1. Jamaican fiction   2. Jamaica – History – Fiction 3. Slavery – Fiction
4. Women slaves – Jamaica
I. Lovejoy, Paul E.   II. Shepherd, Verene A. III. Trotman, David V. IV. Title

813   '   dc21

Contents

List of Illustrations

PREFACE

Although I have no intention of entering into an exordium, I feel unwilling to commit to the press what I have written without a few prefatory remarks. As the world is deluged with epilogues, I shall not add to the number; the only boon I solicit is credit for sincerity of intentions. Being a native of Jamaica and having passed several of my earlier years in the planting line and the last few as a missionary among the negro population of that Island, it must, I presume, be readily granted that my position was one which enabled me to obtain ample and practical knowledge of the circumstances portrayed in the following pages. Although dressed in the garments of romance, the events themselves are all frigid truths, which have either transpired under my own immediate observation or admit of proof which it would be impossible to gainsay or deny.

Many of the abominations of the system against which I have aimed this blow, of which I have had ocular demonstration, delicacy prohibits my holding up to public view. Yet I flatter myself that sufficient has been brought within the range of public vision to show that the features of slavery, under whatever form of government it may exist, are essentially the same: repulsive, degrading, and brutalizing, to the human mind.

Engagements which were imperative, together with severe domestic and personal afflictions, have hitherto prevented my writing on the subject which I have long had at heart and against which I have frequently had occasion to raise my voice. A winter's sojourn in the province of Canada, and the leisure necessarily entailed on an invalid in an algid clime, has at length enabled me to prosecute what I had long intended.

THE AUTHOR, Brandford [sic],
Upper Canada, Jany. 1855.

ACKNOWLEDGMENTS

We could not have completed this project without the assistance of the Jamaica Archives in Spanish Town, the National Library of Jamaica and the West Indies Collection of the Main Library, University of the West Indies, Mona. We are particularly grateful to the former Government Archivist, Elizabeth Williams, for permission to publish material from the Perkins Papers. We would also like to acknowledge the assistance of the following individuals: Ahmed Reid for archival research in Jamaica and London and field work at Greenside Estate in Trelawny and various parts of St. Ann; Erica Haughton of the National Library of Jamaica (and a graduate student at the University of the West Indies, Mona), for assistance with map search at the National Library of Jamaica; Cheryl Le Maitre and Jeff Plante for efforts to track Perkins in Ontario, and Silke Strictrodt for searching the Wesleyan Mission Archives in London. Brenda McComb contributed to the fieldwork at Greenside Estate and made editorial comments on the Introduction, Valerie Facey provided good directions to Mount Hermon Pen as well as hospitality after the visits, and Joyce and Norma Perkins, Cyrus Francis Perkins's great-grand nieces, very kindly gave us interviews on two separate visits to the property.

We are grateful to Lascelle A. Bennett, Ruben Foot and Bevern Foot for several guided tours of Greenside Estate. Thanks also go to Bramwell Shepherd and Lt. Col. Raynor Lazarus (and his family Angel, André and Carmen) for providing suitable transportation, and company, for the various tours of Greenside. Reginald Lazarus and his wife Joyce also accompanied us on the tours. For his meticulous reading of the introduction and scrutiny of the Perkins Family Tree, we thank Richard Small; and for their helpful suggestions concerning the reconstruction of the layout of Greenside Estate, we thank Philip Allsworth-Jones and members of the Jamaica Historical Society who organized a fieldtrip to the estate. Finally, for helping us to ascertain the date of Cyrus Francis Perkins's death, we thank Steven Porter.

The research for this project was funded in part by the Social Sciences and Humanities Research Council of Canada through its Major Collaborative Research Initiatives Programme and is associated with the York/UNESCO Nigerian Hinterland Project at York University and the Text and Testimony Collective at the University of the West Indies.

Lovejoy/Shepherd/Trotman

INTRODUCTION

Cyrus Francis Perkins's 'Busha's Mistress, or Catherine the Fugitive': Historical and Literary Context

Paul E. Lovejoy, Verene A. Shepherd, and David V. Trotman

The Novel

Busha's Mistress, or Catherine the Fugitive: A Stirring Romance of the Days of Slavery in Jamaica by Cyrus Francis Perkins (1813-67) was written in Canada in 1854-55 and first published in Jamaica in twenty installments in the *Daily Telegraph and Jamaica Guardian* (Kingston) in 1911. As the title indicates, the novel relates to the era of slavery when Jamaica was among Britain's most productive sugar-producing colonies, generating considerable wealth from the combination of sugar and slavery. It was a period during which the output of sugar estates far exceeded any other type of agricultural unit in Jamaica; and sugar estates employed a large proportion of the island's enslaved population. The novel belongs to a long literary tradition of the Anglo-Caribbean, and more widely within the British Empire. Indeed, literary works by English writers that focus on England's Caribbean colonies date to the sixteenth and seventeenth centuries, as Thomas Krise's account of the English literary representations of the Caribbean between the age of exploration and the age of abolitionism demonstrates.[1] Among these, notes Krise, were Walter Raleigh´s *Discoverie of Guiana* (1596) and Daniel Defoe's *Robinson Crusoe* (1719).

Literary output increased considerably in the eighteenth century, and included exploration and travel narratives, poetry, descriptive prose, and narrative histories, some by writers born in the region or by longtime residents, mostly white.[2] Olaudah Equiano's *Interesting Narratives* (1789) represents an early literary output by a Black African. In the half century following the publication of Daniel Defoe's *Robinson Crusoe*, the burgeoning trade in African captives brought attention to the expanding population of enslaved Africans in the colonies, and according to Krise, 'changing sensibilities of Britons at home, forced the issue of slavery to the forefront of West Indian literary representations.'[3] The Anglo-Caribbean featured prominently in more than two dozen works of English prose written in the eighteenth century. Black people, though not always enslaved Blacks in the Caribbean, were also the subject of English plays and prose fiction from Shakespeare to Dickens.[4] Thus the period between 1596 and the publication of *Busha's Mistress* was certainly a period with fiction.

Despite this focus, as Ruta Sani has observed, most of this 'considerable exotic writing... about the Negro [sic] in the West Indian scene prior to the twentieth century... cannot be properly considered West Indian literature,'[5] that is, they were not written by individuals from/born in, the Caribbean. Among the few exceptions were J.W. Orderson's *Creoleana* (1842), Maxwell Philip's *Emmanuel Appadoca*, the anonymously authored nineteenth century novel *Adolphus, a Tale* (1854), and Frieda Cassin's *With Silent Thread* (1890).[6] Like these four books, *Busha's Mistress* is an early example of what George Lamming, the Barbadian novelist, describes as 'the West Indian novel,' that is, a novel "written by the West Indian about the West Indian reality," in this case about Jamaica.[7] So while 'belonging to' the long literary tradition of works by English writers that focus on England's Caribbean colonies, it also helps to initiate a new genre of the 'West Indian' novel – contested as that concept is today.[8] There are, of course, other examples of prose narratives and fictional representations of Jamaica as Krise and John Gilmore, among others, have shown. Among the best examples are William Pittis's novella *The Jamaica Lady* published in 1720; *The Fortunate Transport*, published around 1750,[9] the anonymously written *Hamel, The Obeah Man* (1827) and *Marly, or a Planter's Life in Jamaica*, published in London in 1828. Much later, in 1933, Mary Gaunt published *Harmony: A Tale of the Old Slave Days* in Jamaica which deals with slavery on a sugar estate in nineteenth century St. James and so covers some of the same themes as *Busha's Mistress*. However, none of these seems to have been written by Jamaicans or authors born in the Caribbean, though they focused, albeit tangentially (especially in the case of the first two), on Jamaica. Indeed, as Ken Ramchand stresses, it was not until the twentieth century with the publication of Tom Redcam's *Becka's Buckra Baby* (which predated the newspaper version of *Busha's Mistress* by eight years) that novels written in the Creole genre began to proliferate.[10] Evelyn O'Callaghan also notes that "literary accounts of white Creole experience of the West Indies (the Anglophone Caribbean) ... are [still] few and far between".[11] The author of *Marly* claimed to have been a 'slave driver', implying direct knowledge of plantation life in the Caribbean,[12] but he was clearly not a Jamaican. *Busha's Mistress*, the rediscovery of which also raises new questions about the connections among British colonies, in this case Jamaica and Canada, may not have been the first work of fiction in English by someone from the Caribbean, but it certainly must be given a place among the early representations of the 'creole' novel.[13] Whether, as a Creole or 'native', Perkins had any grand intentions of 'decolonizing and indigenizing imaginatively' native cultural traditions, to borrow (and paraphrase) a concept from the editors of *The Routledge Reader in Caribbean Literature*, is open to debate.[14] Indeed, like other pre-1930 Creole writers, Perkins, while seeming to celebrate native cultural traditions and history, does so 'within the context of colonialism'.[15]

The version of *Busha's Mistress* being presented here is a combination of the original manuscript, which survives in poor condition in the Jamaica Archives in Spanish Town, the newspaper version from the *Daily Telegraph and Jamaica Guardian*, and three copies of a typescript of the manuscript made by the author's great-granddaughter, Miss Lilly G. Perkins, apparently after the publication of the newspaper version. The original manuscript and one copy of Miss Perkins's typescript are on deposit in the archives in Spanish Town.[16] Two other copies of the typescript (one draft, one corrected), along with a bound volume of the newspaper serialization are in the National Library of Jamaica.[17] The published version was clearly based on the manuscript that today is in Spanish Town, but it was heavily edited, eliminating certain passages that perhaps were deemed too risqué, as well as altering the text when the manuscript was unclear or parts were missing. It is not known how widely the newspaper version circulated, but the fact that the newspaper, published in Kingston, seems to have survived for less than two years suggests that its circulation was probably scant. Certainly so far, we can tell there is no reference to the newspaper version or the manuscript in the scholarly literature on Jamaica. The current edition is intended to give this novel a wider circulation.

Perkins represents a portion of white Jamaican society of the early nineteenth century that was critical of slavery and the conditions facing people after the abolition of slavery. Some members of the family were affiliated with the evangelical churches that were critical of slavery, and Cyrus Francis and his brother Henry were lay preachers (Cyrus with the Wesleyans). Cyrus Francis Perkins's stance as a [white] native-born critic of slavery is reflected in his 1855 statement that the subject of slavery was a topic which "I have long had at heart and against which I have frequently had occasion to raise my voice". Perkins's attitudes are noteworthy within a context where the majority of residents of European descent in Jamaica were unabashedly pro-slavery. The novel then, provides a critique of slavery that is an interesting reflection of the opinion of those precious

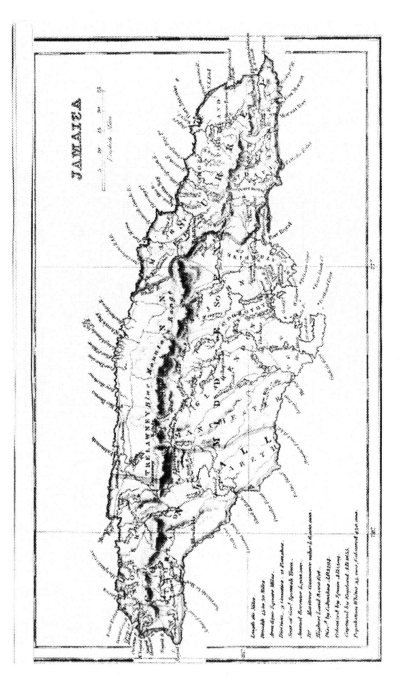

Jamaica in the Early Nineteenth Century

few resident Europeans who found slavery an abomination. This self-identified 'native' view qualifies *Busha's Mistress* as a 'West Indian' or 'Creole' novel, as Lamming defines the term.[18] Indeed Perkins identifies himself as 'a native of Jamaica.' In the preface that was published in the newspaper account, he states that because of this familiarity, "it must, I presume, be readily granted that my position was one which enabled me to obtain ample and practical knowledge of the circumstances portrayed in the following pages." Although it is not possible to determine the origins of Perkins's views on slavery, it appears that the attitudes of his family, his association with the Wesleyans, and his travels to Canada were determining factors.

Although Perkins contemplated writing a novel for some time, he did not actually undertake the writing, or at least the major portion of writing, until the winter of 1854-55. Despite the 'sincerity of [his] intentions,' as he writes in his preface, he had been delayed due to "engagements that were imperative, together with severe domestic and personal afflictions." Certainly the death of his first wife in 1848 must have been one of the 'afflictions' that delayed the project, and it was only in late 1854, when he was in Canada recovering from illness, that he found time to finish the manuscript. The novel, therefore, was not actually written in Jamaica; but as Perkins observed, "A winter's sojourn in the province of Canada, and the leisure necessarily entailed on an invalid in an algid clime, has at length enabled me to prosecute what I had long intended." The preface was signed 'THE AUTHOR, Brandford [sic], Upper Canada, Jany. 1855.' The spelling 'Brandford' is a curious mistake; there is no such place in Ontario, the reference being to Brantford, west of Lake Ontario, in Brant County. Cyrus Francis Perkins had relatives in Brantford, specifically Col. Charles Cranston Dixon, an uncle related to his mother, whose home near the present site of Langley Park was in the town. One of Perkins's sister, Elizabeth, and her husband, George Warren Burton, lived nearby at Hazel Bank Farm at the time he wrote the novel. In all likelihood, Perkins either stayed at his uncle's residence in Brantford or at Hazel Bank Farm, just outside the town. The novel then is not only a previously unrecognized work of Caribbean fiction, but it also has a claim to Canadian status, thereby joining a small corpus of literature written in pre-Confederation Canada and drawing attention to the inter-colonial connections that tied Canada and the Caribbean together.

The relationship between the Caribbean and Canada is of course long standing, rooted as it was in the British Empire and the economic interrelationship between the Caribbean and North America. The

Canadian Atlantic colonies from where the Perkins family originated conducted a brisk trade in salted cod that was exchanged for sugar, molasses and rum.[19] 'Screech' became popular in Canada as a rum product of Newfoundland, using as its base imported Jamaican rum, while salted cod, first imported to feed the enslaved population in Jamaica, became entrenched as a staple of the labouring classes of the post-emancipation period as part of the delectable national dish, ackee and salt fish. These long-standing economic relations even encouraged some thought of political union between the new Canadian confederation of 1867 and selected parts of the Caribbean. Planters in Barbados presented a proposal for entry into the Canadian confederation in 1884; their counterparts in the Leewards proffered similar proposals, and the matter was debated in the Jamaican Legislative Council in the same year.[20] But these proposals were short-circuited not only because of the opposition of the British Colonial Office and the still influential West Indian lobby but also no doubt because of the equally powerful racism of many sections of the Canadian population who feared being swamped by 'hordes of blacks.'

The movement of goods and capital between the two parts of the British Empire, albeit uneven, intensified in the nineteenth century nonetheless; but it was the movement of peoples which would raise problems by revealing the racial dimension which was the distinguishing and most disturbing characteristic of the relationship. The early movement of Jamaican Maroons to Nova Scotia after their expulsion from Jamaica after the Maroon War of 1796 set the stage. Although the Maroons worked on the Citadel and contributed to a network of defense against both French and American incursions, their stay in Nova Scotia was short-lived and leaving the chilly social and geographical climate opted to go to Sierra Leone.[21] Some white Jamaicans, including perhaps some of Perkins's own family, would find refuge in Canada in order to escape what they saw as the inevitable rise of 'Quashie' and the consequent decline of 'civilization' after the abolition of slavery in the British colonies. Others like Perkins himself would use imperial and family connections to acquire an education in Canada, visit for purposes of recuperating health, or simply to find time for creative reflection on their Caribbean home. In this sense, Perkins is perhaps the forerunner of a kind of émigré literature that is now an integral part of the Canadian body of letters.[22]

Besides *Busha's Mistress*, Perkins also dabbled in poetry, some of which, like *Quashie's Lament* and *Donald MacDonald* are among the Perkins Papers in the Jamaica Archives and are reproduced here. It is interesting to note that at the time of his writing, Elizabeth Barrett Browning owned property

14

in Falmouth, although she never visited Jamaica.[23] It is likely that Perkins was aware of her poetry especially since his own poetry, like the novel, is largely derivative of contemporary English literature. Indeed the novel and poetry are products of intra-colonial interaction, in this case between Canada and Jamaica, as well as influences derived directly from Britain. These intra-colonial connections are particularly evident in the life of Perkins. Although born and bred in Jamaica, living there through three marriages and being buried there, he nonetheless retained ties with Canada that were certainly formative in the life of the author if not the subject matter of the novel itself. These ties included connections with his maternal relatives, as well as his father's relatives who lived in Annapolis Royal, Nova Scotia, where his father had been born. As a Jamaican creole, he was a product of the Empire.

More About the Author

Cyrus Francis Perkins was born in Falmouth, Jamaica on January 5, 1813, and was baptized in the Methodist Church in June of the same year.[24] He was the son of William Francis Perkins, a medical doctor attached to the regiment stationed in Falmouth, and Henrietta Perkins (nee Hancorne), daughter of Colonel Hancorne of the same regiment and later a school teacher in Trelawny. Dr. William Perkins, was 'a Canadian of English descent',[25] the son of Francis and Elizabeth Perkins (nee Peck), who had settled in Horton, King's County, Nova Scotia, near Kentville, in 1761. He was one of the three sons of Francis and Elizabeth Perkins, the others being Ely and Cyrus Francis Peck.[26] William studied medicine at the Royal College of Physicians in England, later enlisting in the military. Apparently he was stationed at Cape Coast Castle on the Gold Coast West Africa c. 1800 and is credited in family tradition, at least, with the introduction of vaccination against yaws while serving in West Africa.[27] He came to Jamaica to serve the regiment stationed at Fort Balcarrres in Falmouth. His brothers, Cyrus Francis Peck and Ely remained in Canada. Cyrus Francis Peck Perkins became the Rector of the Anglican Church in Annapolis Royal, N.S., while Ely became a substantial landholder who occasionally visited Jamaica and England. The Rev. Cyrus Peck Perkins apparently died in England in 1817 (five years after a visit to Jamaica in 1812) while yachting at Tor Bay.

A view of Falmouth (from the Church Tower) by Adolphe Duperly, c.1844

Source: University of the West Indies Library. Published in Marcus Binney, John Harris and Kit Martin, *Jamaica's Heritage, An Untapped Resource* (Kingston: The Mill Press, 1991), 14.

Doctor's House, Duke Street, Falmouth

Source: Marcus Binney, John Harris, and Kit Martin,
Jamaica's Heritage, An Untapped Resource
(Kingston: The Mill Press, 1991), 24.

Dr. William Perkins and Henrietta had nine children, five boys (Charles, Cyrus, Henry, Phillip and William) and four girls (Carolyn, Elizabeth, Mrs. E. de St. Remy and a daughter, name unknown, who died in England). Dr. Perkins apparently operated a small medical practice after his retirement from the army. He is listed in the Almanack for some years as the owner of three or four enslaved individuals, almost certainly domestic servants, and two or three livestock, probably horses for his practice. He is never listed as the proprietor of an estate or other property although he lived in Falmouth for over 30 years according to his will deposited in the Island Records Office.[28] He died in 1837.

The author of the novel, Cyrus Francis Perkins grew up in Falmouth, marrying young, raising a family, and experiencing Jamaica during the transitional years from slavery to emancipation. His first wife was Charlotte Jane O'Sullivan from County Cork, Ireland, and they spent the first years of their marriage in Falmouth. Perkins's children by Charlotte were Jane, born in 1830 when he was just 17 years old,[29] Mary (b. 1838) and Robert Simmons Francis (1840-1875).[30] Mary never married. Jane married Charles Smith and their children relocated to Canada, although where is not known. Robert married Sarah Fullager, daughter of another English clergyman who had come out to Jamaica and had become a close family friend. Their son, Robert Cyrus Francis, 'Robin' (1864-1940), married Constance Benaim, and the couple gave birth to Lilly G. Perkins. Lilly, who never married, was responsible for preserving the manuscript of the novel and other family papers, which were eventually deposited in the National Archives in Spanish Town. Hence she is referred to on occasion in this reconstruction of what is known about the life of the author. Perkins's grandson, 'Robin' Perkins bought the 645 acres Lumsden Pen in St. Ann and built a Great House on the property in 1902, which is where Lilly G. Perkins spent the greater part of her childhood.[31]

Cyrus Francis Perkins apparently learned to be a printer, reportedly being trained in all grades of the profession. In 1830, when he became a member of the Methodist Church in Falmouth, he was listed as a printer. Similarly, his occupation was also listed as 'printer' on the baptism records of his daughter, Jane. It is possible that he worked for one of the newspapers that were being published in Falmouth in the 1830s.[32] Later, he appears to have opened a printery in St. Ann's Bay, which his son inherited, although the business proved unprofitable. By the early 1840s, Cyrus Francis Perkins was committed to the Wesleyan movement to the extent that he attempted to become ordained, but instead became the centre of a small controversy; his application was rejected on the basis that he had not been trained in

Britain. According to Robert Stewart, Perkins was a 'native' lay preacher challenging the powers of the Wesleyan mission in Jamaica, seeking but being denied recognition as a native minister in 1842.[33] This failure may have helped form his sensibilities as a Creole. Several of his poems reflect this aspect of being Jamaican. Despite formal rejection for the ministry, he continued as a lay minister. He became closely associated with the missionary work of the Rev. Horace Scotland, 'a parson at [Up Park] camp'.[34] Under his influence, he and Charlotte moved to Westmoreland in the mid 1840s to work with the Wesleyan Mission at Savanna-la-Mar, a sojourn that was tragically interrupted by Charlotte's death. He would later commemorate this event in one of his poems composed after a visit to her grave in 1849.[35] Although never ordained, he nonetheless was referred to as 'Rev.'; at least he is identified as such in the serialized version of *Busha's Mistress*, noting that he had been preoccupied 'the last few [years] as a missionary among the negro population of that Island [Jamaica]'.

After Charlotte died, Cyrus married Mary Maxwell Scotland, widow of his friend, Maxwell Scotland who was the brother of the Rev. Scotland with whom he worked. The couple settled at Devon Pen, along the junction road in the Parish of St Mary. They later sold this property and moved to New England in St Ann's Bay.[36] It is probably in this period that he acquired the printery that later passed to his son. Mary and Cyrus had no children, and when Mary died, he married for a third time to Jane Lloyd Thomson. According to the deed in the Island Record Office, Cyrus Francis Perkins and his third wife, Jane (along with Hugh and John Petrie), conveyed part of New England to one Jasper William Gruber in 1865.[37] The family history is hazy from this point, but Cyrus and Jane then appear to have moved to Mt. Hermon Pen near the White River, also in the Parish of St. Ann. Whether she puchased it or it was given to her by her sister Mary, who was married to Cyrus's brother Henry, is unclear. Norma Perkins believes that all three Lloyd sisters inherited their property: Esther inherited New Market (now Bromley), Jane, Mt. Hermon and Mary, Cottage. What is clear is that Cyrus died at Mt. Hermon in 1867, his obituary noting that he was 54 and that he was survived by his wife, Jane and by three children, presumably those of his first marriage.[38] There are currently two graves at Mt. Hermon, one barely discernible that according to oral history, is Henry's. Why Henry is buried there and not at Cottage is unclear; and whether or not the other one is that of Cyrus Francis Perkins is not known, especially as Lilly Perkins claimed that he was buried at New England. The alternative account is that both couples lived at Mt. Hermon Pen at some point. Mary then appears to have given Mt. Hermon to Jane after Henry died and then she moved to her own property, Cottage Pen. This account would explain why Henry is buried at Mt. Hermon. The other grave would then either be Cyrus's or Jane's.

The Historical Setting of the Novel

Cyrus Francis Perkins was born at the height of the slave system in Jamaica only six years after the abolition of the transatlantic trade in African captives. As the son of a medical doctor in Falmouth, he undoubtedly was exposed to plantation society and intermingled with the families of the urban elite of the town, which at the time was the main port on the north coast of Jamaica and one of the most important colonial towns in the Caribbean. Hence he had intimate knowledge of the rural economy of Trelawny parish, which at the time was based primarily on sugar and slavery. Indeed in the letter to the Governor of Jamaica in the mid-1830s, Perkins states that he had once been an Attorney,[39] and in his Preface, he claims that he had been in 'the planting line', which implicitly meant either owning or managing enslaved people or both. But there is no record that he owned enslaved people himself. Perkins may have acquired his knowledge of 'the planting line' as an 'Attorney', (or book-keeper or overseer) apparently working for the Cunningham family on at least one of their many estates in Trelawny, though he would have been rather young for such a position during the slavery period. Indeed, the Returns of the Registration of Slaves for the years 1817 to 1832 do not list him as 'Attorney' for Greenside. Whatever may have been his position on a sugar estate, he claims in his Preface that

> my position was one which enabled me to obtain ample and practical knowledge of the circumstances portrayed in the following pages. Although dressed in the garments of romance, the events themselves are all frigid truths, which have either transpired under my own immediate observation or admit of proof which it would be impossible to gainsay or deny.

The fact that he identifies Greenside, a sugar plantation overlooking the historic town of Falmouth, as the estate where he situates his 'romance' seems to have been conscious. He specifically refers to Cunningham as the owner of Greenside, which he was, and Lilly Perkins recorded information based on family tradition that he worked at Greenside, though whether during or after slavery is unclear.[40] Living in Falmouth, he clearly was familiar with surrounding plantations and could well have drawn from this knowledge in creating the 'Greenside' of his story. But there is no reason to believe that the basic story does not draw extensively on Greenside.

Greenside sugar plantation was located about 3¼ miles from the town of Falmouth on what was then called 'The Kings Road' (to Martha Brae) and bordered Salt Marsh Wharf, Belfield, Green Park and Maxfield sugar estates.[41] The parish of Trelawny was one of the most important sugar-producing parishes in Jamaica and the foremost sugar parish in the county of Cornwall. The parish was created in 1770 when the large Parish of St. James was divided in two. The division was the result of consistent pressure by the inhabitants of the eastern end of the parish who complained of difficulties in transacting business in Montego Bay. The first name suggested for the parish was 'New Brunswick' in honour of Queen Sophia of Brunswick, the wife of King George I of England, but the name Trelawny was adopted in recognition of the then Governor of Jamaica, Sir William Trelawny. The Parish comprised 352.6 sq. miles, and was the 5th largest parish in Jamaica.[42]

The parish is hilly in sections, but also had large tracts of land suitable for sugar estates. In 1800, the parish had 88 sugar plantations; in 1804, 95 compared with 85 in Hanover, 89 in St James and 70 in Westmoreland.[43] Trelawny's importance as a major sugar-producing parish was dependent on a large population of enslaved Africans. In 1811, the enslaved population was 27,000.[44] In 1821, there were 240 planters in the parish. The population then included 885 whites, 4,893 browns and 21,286 blacks. In 1829, when the parish had 88 sugar estates in operation, the Jamaica Almanack listed 25,654 enslaved people.[45] In 1832, two years before the abolition of slavery, the enslaved population was reported to be 25,196.[46] St Ann, with 24,708 enslaved people came the closest to Trelawny's figure.[47] In 1832 when there were an estimated 527 sugar estates in the island (total number of properties, 960) 49.5 per cent of the enslaved population worked on sugar estates with a sex ratio of approximately 93 males per 100 females.[48] In 1817, the sex ratio of Trawlany's enslaved population was 98.4 males per 100 females, reflecting the fact that almost no new Africans arrived after the abolition of the slave trade in 1807.[49] Nonetheless, a high proportion of the enslaved population had been born in Africa, even as late as 1832. In 1789, the Assembly estimated that 25 percent of the enslaved were Africans, but Barry Higman has argued that this was an underestimation. According to his calculations, ten years after the abolition of the trade in 1817, the proportion of Africans among the enslaved population was still

37 per cent.[50] As the statistics recorded in the *Jamaica Almanack* demonstrate, the demography of Trelawny stabilized in the decades after 1807, when the novel is set.

The estates in the parish of Trelawny acquired many of their enslaved labour force between 1780 and 1807 when at least 354,000 enslaved Africans were brought to Jamaica, although not all remained there, some

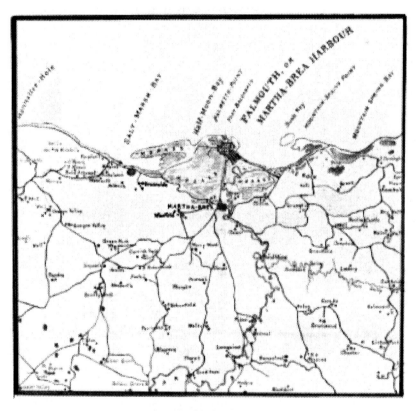

Parish of Trelawny, 1804

Source: James Robertson,
Maps of the Counties of Cornwall, Middlesex and Surrey
(Jamaica, 1804).

being transshipped to the Hispanic mainland or North America. Nonetheless, a profile of the origins of the enslaved population can be fairly reasonably reconstructed for Greenside Estate and the neighbouring areas described in the novel. Many of the people came from the interior of the Bight of Biafra and spoke or were identified as Igbo, and if not, were Ibibio, known in Jamaica as Moco. Many others arriving in this period were from the Gold Coast and therefore were mostly Akan or at least could speak Twi. There was also an identifi able cluster of people from West Central Africa, many coming from Kongo or the interior of the Loango coast. Consequently three ethno-linguistic groups predominated, Igbo/ Ibibio, Akan, and Kongo, and the names recorded in the plantation registry for Greenside Estate notes a predominance of these ethnicities, as reflected in Appendix III.

The information on the African population arriving in Falmouth, from where the enslaved people on Greenside would have been purchased is spotty, available only for five years in the 1790s when 2,356 enslaved Africans are recorded to have arrived. Of these, 34 per cent came from the Bight of Biafra, 30 per cent came from the Gold Coast another 20 per cent came from the Windward Coast, that is the region west of the Gold Coast and largely Sierra Leone and upper Guinea. The Bantu region of West-Central Africa accounted for 10 per cent of those arriving in Falmouth, less than the island as a whole according to the available data.[51] The Falmouth data vary from the pattern for Jamaica, for which information is more complete.[52] Nonetheless, the importance of the Igbo population appears to be confirmed, and it is likely that the Akan were present in disproportionate numbers in Trewlany to those in Jamaica as a whole. References to Myal and obeah in the novel seem to confirm this impression.

Falmouth became the seat of parochial authority in the 1780s, succeeding Martha Brae as the chief town in the Parish. The town was named Falmouth to perpetuate the link with Sir William Trelawny, whose birthplace was Falmouth in the county of Cornwall in England. Falmouth was built on lands previously called Palmetto Point Pen, property of Edward Moulton Barrett, a descendant of the Barretts who were granted an enormous tract of land by Charles II between 1660 and 1670 as a reward for supporting Charles I and the monarchy in the civil war in England in the 1640s. The Barretts owned land that extended from Cinnamon Hill in St James to the border of Trelawny to the east, along the seacoast. Barrett Hall Pen on the border of St James and Trelawny was one of the family residences. At the time of the story, Elizabeth Barrett Browning, a descendant of Edward Moulton Barrett, owned land in Falmouth.[53]

After its establishment as the capital of Trelawny, Falmouth attracted sugar planters who bought land for residences in the town. The richer ones built their houses using imported stones and bricks from England. The not so rich used imported lumber. By the early nineteenth century, Falmouth became famous locally for its two-story stone and brick buildings, a reflection of the prosperity arising from sugar production. In the 1820s and 1830s, its notable buildings included the Anglican cathedral, built in 1796, the Falmouth Water Company and the Iron Foundry. During the height of the sugar industry, Falmouth was known as 'the emporium of the northside', with many Jewish merchants established there.[54] Its busy harbour handled ships unloading plantation supplies, consumer goods, enslaved Africans, foodstuffs, loading sugar and other colonial products to be sent to England. Falmouth became a Free Port in 1805 during the height of the sugar trade in the early nineteenth century and during the period in which the novel is set, was the most important port on the north coast of Jamaica.

When isolated from the other holdings of the Cunningham family, Greenside Estate appears to have been a below average sized plantation in Jamaica, with approximately 600 acres of land and an enslaved population of about 225-250; for Higman's quantitative survey suggests that the average Jamaican sugar plantation was 1,036 acres.[55] However, the combined holdings of the Hon. George Cunningham (who died in 1865) as reported in 1812 was 1,151 enslaved people, 419 livestock and over 1,500 acres of land.[56] George Cunningham also owned the adjacent plantation of Maxfield and The Corner, with their population of 154 enslaved people and 157 stock. His brother, the Hon. James Cunningham owned Biddeford (210 enslaved people, 272 livestock), Hopewell (229 enslaved people, 248 stock), and Marked Cave (236 enslaved people, 139 stock), and another brother, Samuel owned Mason Gang and its 46 enslaved inhabitants and 7 stock, and Roslin-Castle, with 191 enslaved people, 185 livestock. The three brothers together had 1,320 people in slavery and 1,197 head of stock. George Cunningham however was not the largest landowner in Trelawny. That honour went to John Tharp, with 10 properties including Good Hope, valued at £821,530 in 1792[57] when he owned over 2,500 enslaved people.[58] The enslaved population attached to nine of these estates was valued at £187,835.[59]

The layout of Greenside Estate in the period of slavery remains unclear. What has been ascertained from the novel, oral history and the tour of the site, is that it had the usual overseer's house and bookkeeper's cottage, enslaved people's huts, estate dungeon/gaol, hothouse, cane lands, factory

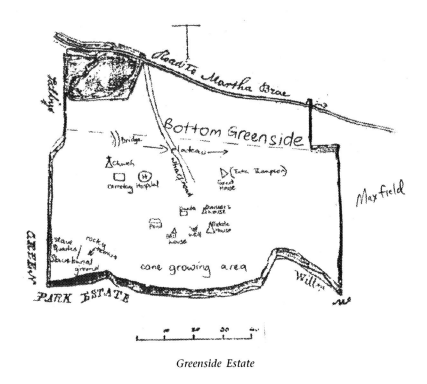

Greenside Estate

Source: Richard Wilson, Private Collection (Jamaica Archives)

buildings and provision grounds. A plan of Salt Marsh Wharf shows the properties on its borders,[60] and a sketch of lands owned by Samuel Barrett deposited in the Island Record Office has details on its size.[61]

In 1832, with 232 enslaved Africans on the property, Greenside conformed to the pattern for Jamaica as a whole, where almost 50 per cent of enslaved people were held in units of more than 150.[62] The number of enslaved workers at Greenside stabilized at 225-230 people. The number of livestock varied to a greater extent: 206 in 1821; 212 in 1823; 228 head in 1824 and a low of 176 on the eve of the Emancipation Act. Although sugar was the principal focus of production, animals were needed for mills, which dictated that there was a sizeable number of livestock on Greenside Estate.[63] In 1832, Greenside Estate was one of 393 sugar plantations in Jamaica with an enslaved population of over 200 when the average number of enslaved people on sugar estates was 223 with a range up to 600.[64]

Ruins - Overseer's house

Ruins - Overseer's house

Ruins - Sugar works

Ruins - Cemetery

Source: Photographs by Paul E. Lovejoy

As absentee proprietors, the Cunninghams only visited Greenside occasionally. Nonetheless, as Perkins remarked in his introductory statements, "very frequently too, some members of the Cunningham family spent holidays at that huge old building at the top of the hill, called by the slaves the 'Great House'."[65] As Perkins begins his novel, the manager, not the proprietor, occupied the house; and this too seems to have been the usual situation. The surviving crop accounts also suggest that the owner was not in residence to manage the property but relied on overseers and on Attorneys. Such 'Attorneys' had no connection with the legal profession but instead were agents for owners, obtaining weekly reports from overseers, making biannual visits to the properties under their care, and submitting annual returns to the proprietors. They were above the overseers in rank and received annual salaries.[66]

Perkins describes Greenside from the vantage point of the post-slavery period when the property was no longer a flourishing sugar estate but a grazing pen for animals. Greenside had always had a large number of livestock but with the demise of sugar, it relied more heavily on livestock, as was generally the case in the Parish of Trelawny. The transition was evident as early as 1836, when the Parish had at least twenty pens.[67] Greenside soon became one of them. According to Perkins's own account of Greenside, 'most of the buildings formerly used in the manufacture of sugar have been dismantled and the materials carried away, while those that remain have sadly suffered from the destructive hand of time.'[68] The former 'Great House' lost its splendour and was eventually torn down. Although some sugar and rum continued to be sold, the estate was forced to cater to the local market for supplies and foodstuffs, earning £1,493.7.0 in 1845, £1,081.10.3 in 1846 and £975.15.0 ½ in 1847, chiefly from the sale of milk, grass, wood, shingles and cattle.[69] By 1851, Greenside was listed in the Crop Accounts with livestock sales of £918.4.9 for 1851-52 and £908 from the sale of livestock, milk and grass in the following year.[70] Cunningham also earned money from rents collected from freed people, resident on the land, with just over £81 collected in 1846.[71] Cottages had been provided for the enslaved, free of cost but freed people had to pay rent. The estate remained in the Cunningham family until it was sold in 1865, by which time it was a far different place from the time of the novel.

The transformation of former sugar estates into livestock farms or 'pens' was a typical development in post-slavery Jamaica when the declining economic conditions of the sugar planter-class and its inability to raise capital to continue in the sugar business, led many to switch to other products that required less capital and labour. The decline in the importance of sugar is revealed in Veront Satchell's quantitative survey which shows that, whereas in 1839 Jamaica had 664 sugar estates in operation, that number fell to 316 by 1867 and 122 by 1900. Between 1839 and 1900, on average, 8.8 per cent of estates were abandoned annually. By 1900, Trelawny had only 25 sugar estates still in operation, down from 84 in 1836,[72] with 29 having been abandoned after 1867.[73] Today Greenside is abandoned, its ruins returning to the forest, only the foundations of buildings, the well, a causeway, and gravesites surviving. It is not clear when the estate ceased to be a cattle pen or when the building materials were removed to other sites. Some of those who currently live on the land raise a few head of cattle. The land was subdivided in the late nineteenth and early twentieth centuries, and since has been sub-divided further. Some of the present occupants, like the Foot brothers, say that their land has been in the family for many generations. Landowners now currently use the land for a variety of purposes. Mr. Lascelle Bennett for example, operates a bar and restaurant (Paradise Grill). Mr. Bevern Foot and his brother, Ruben, raise cattle and farm. There is a bed and breakfast, 'Greenside Villas'.

There is now very little physical evidence of the sugar estate, apart from a few ruins where the sugar factory, old well, the dungeon for the enslaved and overseer's house once stood. The occasional red bricks, pieces of old bottles, pottery and ceramic (delft ware) can be found on the site of the estate. The cemetery has a number of graves, with two virtually intact. According to Bevern Foot, the late Ray Fremmer, the last owner of the former Great House on neighbouring Green Park Estate, took some of the artifacts from Greenside (including the head stones from some of the graves) to Green Park. Other people removed the bricks and stones for use on buildings in various parts of Trelawny. Perkins's rendition of Greenside is therefore the most substantial survival of this once flourishing sugar plantation.

Summary of the Story

In the story, Mr. Jackson is overseer of Greenside Estate - the 'Busha' of the tale. Mr. Vernon comes out from England in a confidential capacity, although outwardly, he is to fill the post of second bookkeeper. He finds a remarkable state of affairs on the estate. Catherine Brown, a coloured (mixed race) girl, is the 'mistress' of the Busha and the manager of his household affairs. The practice by which white men kept enslaved black or coloured women as their 'mistresses' or 'housekeepers' was a well-established one in Caribbean slave systems.[74] From the moment of his arrival, Vernon is struck by the relationship between the Busha and Catherine. Afterwards, he becomes acquainted with the first bookkeeper, Thomas James Randal Sparks, who had a fondness for drinking rum. George Waldy, the millwright has a misunderstanding with one of the estate girls, Mary Ann Peach. This girl is persecuted by the overseer, because she will not enter into a special relationship with him. She is taken from the stocks and is just about to be flogged publicly in a disgraceful manner when Mr. Fleming, the attorney for the English owners of the estate, drives up on a visit and by the interposition of Vernon, stops the flogging. Mary Ann, called up by the attorney, openly denounces the Busha. Her words make Catherine jealous, and she prepares to leave the Busha's quarters with the little child she has borne him. Jackson's efforts to detain her prove futile. She removes to her Aunt Downey's at the 'Great House', the planter's house on sugar estates. Meantime Mary Ann and Phoebe the cook, enter into an animated conversation on the horrors of slavery and the goodness of Vernon. Vernon becomes impressed with a 'pretty mixed race girl who lives with Mrs. Christy'. He enquires of Sparks as to her ancestry and is told that she has 'a dash of the tar brush'- a negative way of referring to her obvious African ancestry.

With the departure of Catherine, everything in the Busha's house goes to ruin, the food being particularly bad. The house girls are punished in every conceivable way, but matters grow steadily worse. Jackson gets into 'blue fits,' and at one time thinks of returning home to Scotland and marrying Molly, the sweetheart of his boyhood. At length he decides to pay a visit to the 'Great House'. Approaching, he hears Catherine singing melodiously. Catherine receives him coldly and shows her jealousy of Mary Ann. Jackson returns home, unsuccessful and dejected. A few days after there is an uproar at the overseer's house. A fracas occurs during dinner. Waldy throws a glass of rum into Jackson's face and the latter hurls a round of beef, which misses Waldy and is seized eagerly by Cato, the dog. The fracas becomes the talk of the kitchen and Mary Ann shows a curious complexity of nature by deeply sympathizing with the Busha. In revenge for what has been done him, Waldy has Mary Ann's two brothers unmercifully flogged, scourged with salt and placed in a vile, evil-smelling dungeon. The possibility of escape seems slim because of the diligence of Quamin, the watchman. Nevertheless, Catherine and Mary Ann, in league with Vernon, devise a plan by making a mask, using brimstone and chain, which scares the life out of Quamin, who leaves his post and runs all over the place, declaring he had seen 'Cudjo's' ghost in the shape of a 'rolling calf'.

Meantime the imprisoned men make their escape; pursuit follows soon. Chapter III closes with a scene of revelry with Jackson as the host. Chapter IV narrates the curious whims of the cruel enslaver, Mrs. Foster, wife of a Falmouth merchant with whom Vernon has gone to stay for the benefit of his health. The chapter describes the sale of enslaved people attended by Vernon and Mrs. Foster's cruelty to the enslaved. Chapter V deals with the travels of Vernon through the island. In St. Ann, he meets a Mr. Hawkins, a planter who because of his newly adopted anti-slavery views, has freed all those he had enslaved, giving them regular employment and wages afterwards. From Hawkins, Vernon learns more of the horrors of slavery. Humorous passages occur in the description of a ride along a mountain road by Vernon and his servant Quinto, in which the latter's fear of ghosts is vividly brought out. After a long ride, Vernon reaches an old estate house where he is kindly received. Passing a night in a country mansion, Vernon is deeply impressed by Miss Secard, the handsome niece of his hostess, a lady advanced in years.

Chapter VI relates how Catherine and her baby sail for England, the former as servant to a Mrs. Arnold. It also relates the ways in which Jackson breaks the monotony of his life by entertaining friends, including Dickens who almost dies from a prank played on him by his host and we get a glimpse into the 'crop over ball' held at the end of the cane harvesting season. The main event in Chapter VII seems to be Vernon learning from Mr. Fleming, the Attorney, that Fleming is the father of the pretty Celeste, a girl who has impressed Vernon considerably. The Attorney tells him a romantic story of his secret wedding and entrusts him with certain proof of paternity to be produced in England after his death. Chapter VII also tells the story of Old William, a sort of 'Missionary slave', who on account of having visited a neighbouring plantation to preach the Gospel to his fellow-enslaved, is flogged and beaten to death. This incident, as we learn in Chapter VIII, causes consternation amongst the enslaved on Greenside; and, invoking the aid of a neighbouring Obeah Man (Magunge), with the help of the intervention of an enslaved black woman, Rosalie, they hold a 'Myal' dance and endeavour to 'catch' the ghost of the dead man. Sparks is promoted overseer of a neighbouring estate, and getting into a drunken quarrel with Granger, he fights a mock duel and is put to bed in the belief that he is dying. He suffers tortures and awakens pretty well next morning. The rest of the chapter relates an expedition against the Maroons, with the enslaved male acting as guide into Maroon country trying to deceive the soldiers in order to give the Maroons time to act.

Chapter IX is about Catherine's experiences in England where after her first mistress died, she was employed by another, Mrs. Christy. We learn more about Mary Ann whose 'busha', Waldy had relocated from Greenside to Wales estate in the same parish, but at a considerable distance from his former abode. With Waldy gone, the new 'Busha' on Greenside was not too kind to Mary Ann. She also had other worries namely, the threat for Waldy's affection and to their 'relationship' by the 'house girls' (enslaved women domestics) on Wales. On one of her return trips to Greenside after visiting Waldy at Wales, she discovers a Maroon plot to attack Wales. She doubles back to warn Waldy, an act that results in her gratuitous manumission. Chapter X follows the story of Jackson after he was discharged as overseer of Greenside by the new Attorney and had fallen on hard times – a condition that was not regarded with a lot of sympathy from some of the other whites who knew him.

The final two chapters relate Mrs. Christy's return from England, her efforts to protect Catherine Brown from being reclaimed by Greenside, Catherine's search for Jackson, the help she received in this endeavour by people such as the freed African Mrs. Fisher (who told her about her capture on the Guinea coast and shipment to Jamaica and the cruelties she endured especially at the hands of a white woman enslaver), Catherine's reunion with the now freed Mary Ann and the eventual success in locating Jackson in Kingston – obviously a happy ending from her (and the author's?) perspective.

Assessment of the Novel

This is a novel about the period of slavery in Jamaica written in the mid-nineteenth century; one that gives an important view of social conditions at the time and is therefore worthy of the attention of a larger audience. Like planter narratives, travel and missionary accounts, anti/postslavery tracts, journals and narratives of the enslaved, novels have some importance as historical texts. An inescapable question, however, is how reliable is this particular novel? Perkins wrote the novel in Canada; and according to his great granddaughter (when errors of historical fact in the mss. novel such as the date of the Gun Hill and its relationship to the 1st Maroon War, were pointed out to her), he had no reference material with him and relied on his memory for historical data like on the Maroon wars.[75] If read alongside contemporary historical accounts of eighteenth century Jamaica at the height of the slave system as well as modern historical accounts, however, the novel appears fairly accurate. These corroborate the information presented on the capture of enslaved Africans in Africa, the culture of the enslaved Africans (Myal, obeah, belief in ghosts), the origins of enslaved African's ethnicity (Igbo and Akan),[76] and adherence of some to the Islamic faith.[77] The novel also chronicles elements of the sugar plantation regime (gender division of labour and the relationship between gender, colour and occupation), plantation management structure, the prevalence of absenteeism, the brutality of control mechanisms (especially after new overseers become 'seasoned' into the ways of a slave system), and the determination of those resisting slavery (including Maroons), anti-slavery activities in the nineteenth century and individual acts of philanthropy, the importance of the sugar culture and the social practices associated with it (for example, the crop over ball).[78] The reference to Maroon activity also reflects Trelawny's preoccupation with escaped captives, especially after the first Maroon war, though the sequence of events may have been fuzzy in the author's mind at the time of writing.

The novel reflects accurately the practice in all Caribbean slave systems of upper and lower managerial white males forcing enslaved coloured domestic women into 'housekeeper' roles that included sexual 'favours' to 'Bushas'. These unequal sexual unions invariably resulted in 'coloured' (mixed race) progeny, and while some of these children were eventually freed, many others remained enslaved. This pattern is clearly reflected in a conversation between Catherine and Vernon. Asked "was your baby born free?", Catherine responded to Vernon "No, sir, it belong to the property."[79] Unfortunately, even if this is excused on the grounds that this is fiction, the novel glamorizes the position and status of coloured women in slave systems in which rape and other forms of physical and mental torture characterized their lives. The very title is problematic; for what Perkins characterizes as 'romance' is very much open to debate, especially as such 'romance' occurred within the context of a slave system in which there was no equality between enslaved and enslaver. Could these liaisons between enslaved and enslaver, the powerful and the subaltern, be characterized as 'romantic'? How believable is Perkins's avowed anti-slavery/pro-freed black sentiments and actions? How could an anti-slavery activist find, even through the medium of fiction, 'a stirring romance' in a system that sanctioned white men's appropriation of the bodies of enslaved women? The novel will, however, give support to those who exaggerate coloured women's 'independence and autonomy' under slavery and their alleged 'influence' with empowered white men.

33

But we must be careful not to judge the author too quickly by standards and sentiments now taken for granted. The author's voice is believable only in so far as he attempts to accurately portray the sentiments of his time. Very few of even the most progressive abolitionists and anti-slavery proponents advocated equality beyond a notion of equality before a Christian God: cultural or social equality would have been considered too radical. The most benign of the white anti-slavery advocates of the mid-nineteenth century including those who resided in the Caribbean and saw their role as protectors of their less advanced 'brothers and sisters'. They could not escape the patriarchal attitudes of their times any more than they could escape the paternalistic notions which would increasingly separate white anti-slavery liberals from the proponents of a less subtle and more virulent racism. And certainly Perkins does not escape being stamped by his times.

Cyrus Francis Perkins was born into a society that for at least a century and a half had developed ideas, attitudes and behaviour which reflected and supported a dehumanizing system of racial slavery whose *raison d'être* was profit. This system of racial slavery both demanded for its survival and produced in the course of its development an external orientation, particularly on the part of its elites, which inhibited that inward looking gaze which was crucial to the emergence of a Creole sensibility and practice. External economic linkages and dependence were accompanied by external cultural dependence and orientation. But moreover and more importantly this orientation had a deleterious impact on the creative imagination and on literary production in the colonial society. It in part explains the insignificance of creative writing in the period of enslavement and for most of the nineteenth century – insignificant not merely quantitatively but more importantly qualitatively.[80] Perkins's novel and his poetry are among the rare, surviving literary documents of a slave system.

When legal enslavement ended in 1834 the author was a young man of twenty-one. His attitudes and ideas were generated during the period of slavery, although his father was not a substantial enslaver, and therefore his family not wealthy by the standards of those who measured wealth according to the investment in, and profits generated by, the sugar plantation. His travels to Upper Canada exposed him to abolitionist views, as did his association with the Methodists in Jamaica. His brother-in-law, E. de St. Remy, conducted a report on 'Negroes in Toronto' that recommended to the Government of Lord Sydenham social policies that were intended to integrate the expected influx of black refugees from the United States into Canadian society.[81] Perkins saw his role as assisting the formerly enslaved population through the period of apprenticeship and beyond, and hence his lay ministry in Savanna-la-Mar, and also reflected in his novel and poetry. Perkins on his sojourn in Canada, in 1855, aged forty-two, reminiscing on the slavery of his younger days, could claim long held anti-slavery sentiments but his cultural inheritance had ill-prepared him for writing a significant creole romance or novel. The literary tradition in Jamaica was still heavily dependent on Europe for its inspiration for the form of its literary products even if its content was based on the local social environment. And in Perkins's case, he probably was strongly influenced by what he read in Upper Canada.

The author was also operating with a nineteenth-century understanding of 'romance 'which must be distinguished from the more popular use of the term in the twentieth century. As a literary form the romance is defined as a prose narrative treating imaginary characters involved in events remote in time or place and usually heroic, adventurous or mysterious. Moreover the events or incidents are usually invented or exaggerated, often even improbable and marked by strange coincidences. Although the focus is on one major action or character, the romance is multi-episodic with the main character often momentarily 'lost' amidst a bewildering cast of minor characters and events before the author eventually reveals the moralistic denouement. The fact that events may involve love affairs, intimate interactions or romantic liaisons was not the defining characteristic of the form.

The 'romance' was characterized by its attempts to portray 'a world suggestive of a reality within or beyond the real world'. This is what distinguished it from that other prose narrative form slowly coming into its own in the nineteenth century, namely the novel with its particular concern for realism. According to Quinn, nineteenth-century writers who identified their work as a 'romance' did so in order to avail themselves of certain latitude in imagination and construction not necessarily available if the work was described as a 'novel'.[82] Cyrus Francis Perkins writing in 1855 was caught between the dominant literary traditions of the time, namely romanticism, which is also revealed in his poetry, which was then the dominant strain of the movement, but his location of his story in Jamaica also aligned his fiction with the emerging realist concerns of the novel.

There is no mythic past to which Perkins could refer in the Caribbean that was his raw material. The indigenous population whose myths and exploits might have provided grist for the imaginative mill of the writer had been almost decimated and the landscape had been reconstructed to accommodate the plantation and its supporting institutions with its imported inhabitants of Europeans and Africans. With the implantation of that socio-economic construct came the creation of a new society characterized by a brutal racial slavery and in which colour, ethnicity and gender were important factors in the distribution of social roles. Perkins attempts through romance to explore and be intimate with the Creole language, myths, stories and inner lives of the enslaved population. His predecessors and many of his contemporaries were unwilling to attempt this; but to Perkins's credit he tried. In the cold of a Canadian winter Perkins faced the brutal reality of racial slavery 'dressed in the garments of romance'.

Whether the events related in the novel bear any resemblance to the author's personal experiences while 'in the planting line' in western Jamaica remains unclear. Was he the young seemingly anti-slavery second bookkeeper Vernon? Was he the Busha of the novel? Obviously, though, he had first-hand knowledge of the intimate workings of a slave system, before amelioration and abolitionism undermined its survival. He had been a marginal player on the fringe of planter society and became an anti-slavery activist. As a result, Perkins must be given some credibility as an author of nineteenth-century Jamaica and as a participant of the Creole tradition. The novel should be accorded a place within the larger historical and fictional literature of the Caribbean and indeed of Canadian and Commonwealth literature too.

Folio from Busha's Mistress

Source: Lilly Perkins Papers, 4/26/6, Jamaica Archives

Endnotes

1   Thomas Krise, ed., *Caribbeana: An Anthology of English Literature of the West Indies, 1657-1777* (Chicago, 1999). Also see M. Keith Booker and Dubravka Juraga, *The Caribbean Novel in English: An Introduction* (Kingston, 2001) and Alison Donnell & Sarah Lawson Welsh, eds., *The Routledge Reader in Caribbean Literature* (London & New York, 1996), pp. 13-16.

2   Perhaps the most prominent of the narrative histories was Edward Long's *The History of Jamaica*, published in three volumes in 1774 in London by T. Lowndes. Other examples include Matthew Gregory ['Monk'] Lewis's, *Journal of a West India Proprietor Kept During a Residence in the Island of Jamaica* (London, 1834), and Maria Nugent's, *Journey of a Voyage to, and Residence in, the Island of Jamaica, 1801-1805* (London, 1839). See Martin Mordecai and Pamela Mordecai, *Culture and Customs of Jamaica* (Westport CN, 2001), 114-17.

3   Krise, ed., *Caribbeana*, 5.

4   Norman McCollough, *The Negro in English Literature* (Ilfracombe, 1962).

5   Ruta Sani , 'A Bibliographical Survey of the West Indian Novel' (M.A. thesis, Michigan State University, 1972), 4.

6   Written by a Barbadian, Trinidadian and Antiguan/Barbudan respectively. John Gilmore claims that Creoleana, not *Emmanuel Appadoca* (as he said was claimed in the 'Preface' to Selwyn Cudjoe's new edition of this novel published in Amherst, MA, 1997, pp. xiii-xiv), should be accorded the signifi cance of being the earliest novel of the Anglophone Caribbean. See his 'Introduction' to his edited *Creoleana and The Fair Barbadian and Faithful Black* (Oxford: Macmillan, 2002), p. 2.

7   Lamming, *The Pleasures of Exile* (London, 1960), 68.

8   See Gilmore's Preface in Cassin's 1890 novel *With Silent Thread*. Orig. pub 1890 (Oxford, 2002). Bridget Brereton and her co-editors must be thanked for bringing to our attention four Trinidadian novels published between 1838 and 1907. Two of these (Adolphus and Rupert Grey) were authored by Creoles. See 2003 Catalogue of the UWI Press.

9   Krise, ed., Caribbeana, p. 13.

10 Ken Ramchand, *The West Indian Novel and its Background* (London, 1970), 3. Tom Redcam's 1903 novel was followed by those of other Jamaicans: H.G. deLisser (1878-1944); Claude McKay (1890-1948) and Roger Mais (1905-1955). The first half of the twentieth century also features the literature of Dominican writer, Jean Rhys (1894-1939), whose first novel was published in 1939.

11 In Cassin, *With Silent Thread*, 3. Cassin is believed to have been a white Creole in Antigua.

12 As only enslaved people held the position of driver, the author was clearly using this term in a metaphorical sense to indicate involvement in the exploitation of enslaved people.

13 Among such early examples is E.L. Joseph's, *Warner Arundell, The Adventures of a Creole* (London, 1838, and reprinted with introduction by Lise Winer,

University of the West Indies Press, 2001). Unlike Perkins, however, Joseph was not born in the West Indies.

14   Donnell & Welsh, eds., *The Routledge Reader*, p. 4.

15   Ibid., p. 27.

16   Private Deposits, Perkins, L.G. 4/26/6 and 4/26/7, National Archives, Spanish Town.

17   National Library of Jamaica, MS. 194.

18   Also see Edward [Kamau] Brathwaite, *The Development of Creole Society in Jamaica, 1770-1820* (Oxford, 1971).

19   On Canadian-Caribbean trade see Harold A. Innis, *The Cod Fisheries: The History of an International Economy* (Toronto, 1954); Hugh Barry-King and Anton Massel, *Rum – Yesterday and Today* (London, 1983).

20   See Charles Spencer Salmon, *The Caribbean Confederation* (London, 1888); Robin Winks, *Canadian-West Indian Union: A Forty Year Minuet* (London, 1968); and Eric Williams, *From Columbus to Castro–The History of the Caribbean, 1492-1969* (London,1970), 404-405.

21   On the Maroons in Canada, see Robin Winks, *The Blacks in Canada* (Montreal and Kingston, 1997) and Allister Hinds, 'Deportees in Nova Scotia': The Jamaican Maroons, 1796-1800', in Verene A. Shepherd, ed., *Working Slavery, Pricing Freedom: Perspectives from the Caribbean, Africa and the African Diaspora* (Kingston, 2002), pp. 44-68.

22   Changes in a racially biased immigration policy facilitated the increase in the number of non-white visitors and immigrants from the Caribbean in the twentieth century who could contribute to both Caribbean and Canadian literature. The list of authors who have contributed to the fiction written by Caribbean émigrés in Canada in the twentieth century includes Austin Clarke, Dionne Brand, Neil Bissondath, Cecil Foster, Shani Mootoo, Althea Prince, and Makeda Silvera, whose works have strengthened both Canadian and Caribbean letters by their reflections on the homes they have left and the societies they have adopted.

23   Ed Kritzler, 'The Poet and the Preacher: Falmouth's Curious Heritage', Skywriting Magazine, February 2001, 30-34.

24   IRO, Trelawny Copy Register of Baptisms, Marriages and Burials, Vol. 1, 1770-1839.

25   Lilly Perkins Papers Correspondence, MST. 1784.

26   Extract from an 1886 letter from Edmund Cogswell of Nova Scotia to Robert Cyrus Perkins; see Jamaica Archives, 21/3 (197), 4/26/2/7; and Lilly G. Perkins, 'Extracts from letters written by my father, Robert Francis Perkins', Perkins Gifts and Deposits, Jamaica Archives, 4/26/2/23.

27   In an undated fragment of a letter to the Governor of Jamaica, apparently in the 1830s, Cyrus Francis Perkins wrote, 'Although born in Jamaica my relations were English, my father a member of the [Royal College] of P. [Physicians] in London; at an early period of his [career] was stationed at Cape Coast Castle with the garrison (introduced vaccination) from thence he proceeded to this island, & had the honour of attending professionally his Excellency Sir Ayre Coote [1801-1808]. My father had a brother who was for many years Rector

of Annapolis [Royal] in Nova Scotia.' L.G. Perkins Papers, Correspondence, 4/25/6. Also see Lilly Perkins, 'Family History', Perkins Papers, 21/3 (197).

28　Island Records Office (IRO), Trelawny Copy Register of Baptisms, Marriages and Burials, Vol. 1, 1770-1839.

29　The Falmouth Methodist Society's Baptism records for 1838 show that Jane William Perkins was born on September 20th 1830 and baptized on September 5th 1838; see Falmouth Leaders' Meetings, Jamaica Archives, 5/60/5/1, #315.

30　Lilly Perkins Papers, 4/26/2.

31　The Great House, 'Lumsden House', is still standing. The property, which is five miles from Claremont, took its name from the original owner, a Scotsman, William Lumsden. See Lilly Perkins to Elizabeth Causewell of the Georgian and Jamaican Historical Society, March 28, 1977. It is now owned by Neville and Nadine Thompson who bought it in 1981 from Ken and Darcy Wright. There were three previous owners: Charlie Snipe, Henry Stephenson and John Harker. The Perkins family sold the house in 1936 and moved to a small cottage in Claremont. (Interview with the Thompsons on a field trip to Lumsden on 16th March 2001).

32　Notes by Lilly G. Perkins scribbled in her copy of Dan Ogilvie, *History of Trelawny* (Kingston, 1954) 115; Ogilvie had access to the Trelawny Vestry Minutes. These are no longer available. Also see undated fragment of letter from Cyrus Francis Perkins to the Governor of Jamaica, where he refers to his occupation as printer in the period after 1834 (Jamaican Archives, 21/3 (197), Ref 4/26/2/8).

33　Robert Stewart, Religion and Society in Post-Emancipation Jamaica (Knoxville, 1992). We have not been able to trace this incident in the Wesleyan Methodist Missionary Society Archives, SOAS, London. Perkins is not listed in the index to correspondence for Jamaica nor does his name appear in the 'Special Series: Biographical' or the Miscellaneous Papers.

34　Lilly Perkins to Ms. Silvera of the National Library of Jamaica, Sept. 12, 1976.

35　Fuertado Manuscript to Official and Other Personages, cited in Althea Silvera, Acting Head Research, the Institute of Jamaica, to L.G. Perkins, September 7 1976.

36　Lilly Perkins, 'Extracts from letters written by my father, Robert Francis Perkins.'

37　Island Records Office, Twickenham Park, St Catherine, Deeds Liber 946, fol. 20.

38　*The Colonial Standard and Jamaica Despatch* (Thursday, September 19, 1867, p. 2) reported: 'DIED At his Residence, Mount Hermon Pen, Saint Ann, Cyrus Francis Perkins, Esqr., in the 54th year of his age, leaving a wife and three children to lament their loss.'

39　Fragment of letter from Cyrus Francis Perkins to Governor of Jamaica, c. mid-1830s, Perkins Papers, Correspondence, 4/25/6.

40　According to Lilly Perkins ('Family History'), 'He seems to have had a good deal to with plantership & was Att: for Greenside Estate.... [and] He must have lived intimately on a sugar estate to have known so much of the inside life and workings among the subordinate staff. He probably worked on an estate in his youth.'

41 Information in the Island Records Office indicates that 615 acres of Greenside estate were transferred from Robert McGhie to William Tynmore in the eighteenth century. Tynmore appears to have later sold the estate to Samuel Barrett, who in turn sold it to George Cunningham. According to legal records, Samuel Barrett sold 600 acres of Greenside to George Cunningham on October 17th 1817 for £2,422. See Wilson Private Collection. Richard Wilson was Director of the Falmouth Water Company in 1841, and with his brother, Robert M., were land surveyors. The plan of the estate in the Wilson Collection dates from 1801.

42 Ogilvie, *History of Trelawny*, 5-7.

43 The county of Cornwall had 375 sugar estates in that same year compared to 275 in Middlesex and 190 in Surrey. For Jamaica as a whole, there were 830 estates.

44 Ogilvie, *History of Trelawny*, 19.

45 Ogilvie, *History of Trelawny*, 150.

46 The total enslaved population on the island was 312,876; Ogilvie, *History of Trelawny*, 53.

47 Ogilvie, History of Trelawny, 53.

48 B.W. Higman, *Slave Population and Economy in Jamaica, 1807-1832* (Cambridge, 1976), 72.

49 Higman, *Slave Population*, 13, 16

50 Higman, *Slave Population*, 75.

51 David Eltis, Stephen Behrendt, David Richardson, and Herbert Klein, *The Atlantic Slave Trade: A Database on CD-Rom* (Cambridge, 1999).

52 Enslaved Africans were brought to Jamaica during the period of Spanish colonization from 1494 to 1655 and continued to be brought to the island after being seized by the English in 1655, but few enslaved Africans arrived after British abolition in 1807.

53 Kritzler, *The Poet and the Preacher*, 30.

54 Ogilvie, *History of Trelawny*, 34.

55 Jamaica Archives, Noel Wilson Collection, 7/131/12. In the intervening years, 15 acres had been transferred to a small proprietor, William McDonald.

56 *Jamaica Almanack*, 'Return of In-Givings Proprietors, Properties, &c. Given to the Vestries List of properties for 1811', p. 188.

57 Verene Shepherd, 'Pens and Pen-keepers in a Plantation Society', PhD Dissertation, University of Cambridge, 1988, 201-2.

58 Ogilvie, *History of Trelawny*, 147.

59 Shepherd, 'Pens and Penkeepers', 202.

60 National Library of Jamaica, Maps and Plans Collection, T22.

61 IRO, 1126/2000, Liber 665, folio 236 and Noel Wilson Collection, Jamaica Archives 7/131/12.

62 Higman, *Slave Population*, 69.

63 *Jamaica Almanack*, 1821, p. 125.

64 Higman, 'The Spatial Economy of Jamaican Sugar Plantations: Cartographic Evidence from the 18th and 19th Centuries', *Journal of Historical Geography*, 13 (1987), 24.

65 Paragraph 3, Chapter 1. George Cunningham died in August 1865 and at the time was the Custos of Trelawny. Ogilvie, *History of Trelawny*, p. 79.

66 Jamaica had some influential and wealthy Attorneys, the best -known being Simon Taylor, who owned Prospect Pen, the present Vale Royal, official residence of Jamaica's Prime Ministers.

67 See Shepherd, 'Pens and Penkeepers', 67; and Shepherd, 'Questioning Creole: Domestic Producers in Jamaica's Plantation Economy', *Caribbean Quarterly*, 44, 1 & 2 (1998), 93-107.

68 Shepherd, 'Questioning Creole'.

69 Jamaica Archives, Crop Accounts vols. 89, 1845, f. 63; 90, 1846, f. 201; 91, 1847, f. 174.

70 Jamaica Archives, Crop Accounts vol. 95, f. 118, 1853/54.

71 Accounts Current, Jamaica Archives, 1846-47. These accounts indicate that the property collected £60 in rents from freed-people in 1846/47.

72 Based on Stipendiary Magistrates' returns, 1836. See Shepherd, 'Pens and Penkeepers', p. 67.

73 Veront Satchell, *From Plots to Plantations* (Mona, 1990), 42.

74 One of the most infamous examples is that of Thomas Thistlewood and Phibbah. See Douglas Hall, *In Miserable Slavery: Thomas Thistlewood in Jamaica, 1750-1786* (London, 1989).

75 Correspondence between Lilly Perkins and Glory Robertson of the Jamaican Historical Society, Dec. 18, 1968 and Dec. 7, 1968. NLJ, MS. 2019.

76 See chapter VII, last page.

77 Perhaps there is a hint in chapter XI where Mary Ann greeted Catherine, 'bestowing all the benedictions of the east'.

78 See, for example, Higman, *Slave Population*; Brathwaite, *Development of Creole Society in Jamaica*; and Verene A. Shepherd & Hilary McD. Beckles, eds. *Caribbean Slavery in the Atlantic World* (Kingston, 2000).

79 Chapter I.

80 See Ramchand, *The West Indian Novel* 32-38; Kamau Brathwaite, 'Creative Literature of the British West Indies during the Period of Slavery', *Savacou*, I (1970) , 46-74; Michael Gilkes, *The West Indian Novel* (Boston,1981), 9-11; Nana Wilson-Tagore, *Historical Thought and Literary Representation in West Indian Literature* (Gainesville, Florida, 1998).

81 Edward de St. Remy, 'Report on the Toronto Negroes', National Archives of Canada, Governor-General's Office, Miscellaneous Records, Lieutenant-Governor's Correspondence, Upper Canada, 1835-1841, Rg7, G14, vol. 5, microfilm reel H-1178, pp. 2193-2202. Also see Lord Sydenham dispatch, No. 52, April 24, 1841, Public Record Office, CO 42/478; and Donald G. Simpson, *Under the North Star: Black Communities in Ontario before 1870* (New Brunswick, NJ: Africa World Press, 2005).

82 On romance see Edward Quinn, *A Dictionary of Literary and Thematic Terms* (New York, 1999).

ONE[1]

*W*hoever knows anything of the town of Falmouth, in the Island of Jamaica, as a matter of course must know Greenside Estate. Its remarkable entrance, standing directly on the road leading to Montego Bay; the mossy ornamental pillars, with a handsome lodge for the watchman on either side, all of white limestone having been once seen could hardly be forgotten. Besides, on this property, is the celebrated gunhill, with its sugar-loaf top towering to the clouds, which for generations past has been a noted land-mark for the mariner, and was the rallying point of the Maroons in one of their engagements with the troops and militia.

This well known hill derived its name from the circumstance of two cannon having been found on its pinnacle, but whether they were placed there during the Maroon War, or long antecedent to that event, to mark the grave of the celebrated Bradshaw, who figured in the reign of Cromwell, as is roundly asserted by Bridges the great Annalist of Jamaica, has never been determined; one of the guns which was removed several years ago, bears neither date nor inscription. Greenside is now merely a grazing pen, most of the buildings formerly used in the manufacture of sugar have been dismantled and the materials carried away, while those that remain have sadly suffered from the destructive hand of time; but at the date to which our story looks back, this property was in a high state of cultivation and its produce stood unrivalled in the British market; very frequently, too, some of the members of the Cunningham family spent the holidays at that huge old building at the top of the hill, called by the slaves the 'Great House' when its now solitary courtyard was frequently filled with gay equipages, and the long range of stables were occupied by studs of blood and metal. Yes! that now desolate old house had then its banquet hall and 'the harp and the viol, the tabret [tabour][2] and pipe, and wine were in the feast'. Brilliantly the lights shone from those elegant chandeliers, over which the spider now weaves his web, and merry peals of laughter rang through that stately sitting-room with its gilded cornices, its richly variegated floor, and its large handsome mahogany folding doors. Nor did the portals then wear such a sombre hue. No, they looked bright and fresh as the morning. But why dwell on this old house and its mouldering grandeur?

The crop had been taken off and if there could be such a thing as leisure connected with slavery it might have been expected at this season; but yet it was toil, toil, toil, with nothing to break the dull monotony save the crack of the driver's whip which ever and anon broke on the car like the distant report of a pistol. It was at this time that Mr Vernon arrived at Greenside and having presented certain credentials, bearing the well known signature of the Attorney, to Mr Jackson, the overseer, was coldly invited to a seat on the old green bench which graced the piazza of Busha's house. This house must not, however, be confounded with the 'great house' mentioned before: the buildings stood a mile apart. The former was appropriated entirely to the use of the proprietor, attorney or their friends: the latter was the residence of the manager for the time being. Near the overseer's domicile there was a range of rooms known as 'the barracks'. In this the bookkeepers and white mechanics connected with the estate resided. Jackson having learnt from a perusal of the letters that Vernon was to be installed as second bookkeeper, gave a shrill whistle, whereon four dogs, three mulatta girls, two black boys, and an old man, simultaneously made their appearance. The canine favourites looked up and opened their mouths, a liberty which the slaves seemed afraid to take, even when Busha demanded, 'what the d—l they had all been doing since dinner'. He ordered one of the girls 'to call Miss Brown', and the others to 'go to h-ll'. Whether the latter order was, or was not obeyed, is, of course, problematical. The former, however, was speedily executed, and Miss Brown, Busha's reputed wife, responded to the call. Miss Brown was a quadroon of prepossessing appearance. There was a dignity in her demeanour which formed a striking contrast with the servile spirit of her fellow slaves and at once convinced the beholder that she maintained a very different position in the overseer's household. Her hair was dark and fell in natural ringlets on her shoulders, her round black eyes would have conveyed the idea of boldness, had it not been that they fell suddenly to the floor on their gaze being met. She was dressed in a gingham gown and shoes without stockings, a silk handkerchief thrown across her shoulders completed her costume, a string of coral beads adorned her neck, a pair of gold earrings dangled in her ears, and a pair of bright scissors and a thread housewife at her side. The overseer, after a few enquiries, ordered Miss

Brown to provide a room for the second bookkeeper, and without saying anything to Vernon, rode off to the fields.

Our young friend having finished a very intent survey of the works connected with the property, which were erected in the vicinity of the dwelling house, determined to make an effort to scrape acquaintanceship with Miss Brown, who had taken a seat on a low chair which stood nearby behind a door left ajar.

'That child is yours? Is it not, my good woman,' he enquired.

'Yes, sir, I is its mother, sir,' she replied.

'Was your baby born free?' further enquired Vernon.

'No, sir; it belong to the property,' replied Miss Brown.

'Does the overseer treat you kindly?' asked Vernon.

Miss Brown now rose from her seat, took a survey of the staircase and the yard, apparently to ascertain if the coast was clear. She then resumed her seat and said: 'You is a newcomer, sir, and you don't know nothing yet. If Busha hear you ask me anything he will be vex. Bokra-sah on the estates never allowed to talk to the negroes; if Busha knows of such a thing he always sends them away,' replied Miss Brown.

'But I shall always speak kindly to the slaves; I pity them, and I hope we shall be good friends,' said Vernon.

'Yes, sir; the other bookkeeper, when he ins fus come from Englan' was kind hearted, but now he is 'most as 'pitiful as them other. Mr Jackson use to treat the negroes well as first, but now he is too hard 'pon them,' replied Miss Brown.

Someone came in before Vernon replied, and Miss Brown retreated into a corner, evidently wishing to avoid conversation which she thought hazardous with a stranger.

The overseer had ridden over to a neighbouring property on an evening's visit, and had not returned when Vernon was conducted to the bookkeeper's barracks by a little black boy, who, having set down the candlestick on a kind of crotchety article that answered as a table, quickly departed, leaving the new bookkeeper to choose whether he would go to bed or remain sitting on the little three legged stool, that seemed to claim near affinity to the rickety table. Vernon, for the present, chose the latter, and began leisurely to contemplate his apàrtment. It was a room about twelve feet square, the walls had once been whitewashed, but in consequence of the repeated 'smoking out' of mosquitoes, they had now become of a dingy brown. In one corner stood a pine bedstead surrounded by a dirty checkered net. A large bag filled with brash from the plantain tree answered for a mattress. This was covered with two clean oznaburghs

[sic] sheets and a dirty blanket. In the opposite corner stood a musket with fixed bayonet, and the dilapidated table which seemed to say to the wall, 'united we stand, divided I fall'. Vernon had never before spent a night in such a cheerless looking room, nor had he ever rested on such a couch. However, he had an object in view, in the execution of which he was prepared to make considerable sacrifice.

The great majority of young men who have from time to time migrated to the colonies in the British West Indies, have been needy adventurers, whose sole object was to gain wealth. This desire attained, they hastened back to their fatherland to enjoy the good fortune that had crowned their exertions. This was the hope that animated the West Indian planter – from the bookkeeper feeding the hogs in his mudbespattered pantaloons, to the attorney who had the entire management of twenty or thirty properties. But Mr Vernon was not of this class; he was the only son of a wealthy gentleman proprietor of some plantations in Antigua. Mr Vernon, senior, having become convinced that his total ignorance of agriculture as pursued in tropical countries, constantly subjected him to imposition, was anxious that his son should have a practical knowledge of West India estates. The son was pleased at the idea of visiting distant lands, and notwithstanding [the fact that] his mother entertained many very serious fears of yellow fever, hurricanes and earthquakes, young Vernon sailed for Jamaica, having been furnished by Mr Cunningham with a letter to his attorney, Mr Fleming, desiring that every facility should be afforded him of obtaining, not only a knowledge of the manufacture of those great staples, sugar and rum, but also of the minor products of the country. This was the primitive object that led Vernon to visit the Western isles. Having, however, heard a great deal from a fellow passenger of the cruelties perpetrated on the slaves, he landed prejudiced in their favour. These impressions were strengthened and confirmed by ocular demonstration, and most of the feelings that had influenced his mind on leaving home became merged in those of the philanthropist. Imbued with a determination to act in this character during his residence in the country, he felt convinced that his alliance with planting or the planters, would not be very close. These and other thoughts, past, present, and future, engaged his mind as he lay ruminating on his humble bed of straw.

Having furnished our readers with an inventory of the philanthropical bookkeeper's chamber, he will not be surprised that 'balmy sleep' fell not suddenly on him, especially when we add that the 'smoking out' had been omitted, and that the mosquitoes knew their way through holes in the checkered net even in the dark. At length the struggle between exhausted nature and unsatisfied insects was about to end in favour of the former, when his attention was arrested by voices in the adjoining room.

'You know, Mass George, Busha is put me in de bilbo agen, an 'e keep me da whole week,' said a voice evidently feminine.

'He put you in the stocks?' replied the individual addressed, in an angry tone; 'then d-m him, he shall pay for it.'

'Now,' answered the first speaker, 'tis jis so you always go on, you neber can keep your temper; you no member sah me is belangst to de estate and Busha is Busha – de mo you buse him, de mo'e will prosecute me. You no member Mr Percy gal?'

'Well then,' replied the person addressed as Mass George, 'I won't say anything more. Now for the supper.'

After some preliminary arrangements supper seemed to be ready. Talking continued, but Vernon, unwilling to play the eavesdropper, managed to fall asleep.

Our adventurer was up with the sun in the morning. As he went forth he could not but admire the loveliness of the scene. The feathered tribe poured forth in lively cadence their dulcet notes, the dewdrops glittered on every leaf, and the air was pregnant with the rich perfume of the orange blossom. The works of nature were calculated to delight the senses and cheer the heart. But, alas! what a gloomy contrast they formed with the moral degradation that everywhere stalked forth with its brazen front. While these reflections passed in the mind of Vernon he was summoned to the morning meal by one of the house girls who roared at the pitch of her voice, 'Bookkeeper, brekfus' ready.' On entering the house he encountered Miss Brown, who looked full at him with her round, black eyes, and the next instant cast their glance on the floor.

The breakfast room of the overseer's house was exquisitely clean, the floor highly polished. The walls had been painted sky-blue, but were now much faded. Against them hung several prints representing the famous battle of Trafalgar; the window curtains were as white as soap and water could make them, and, in short, everything reflected great credit on the management and housewifery of the 'Busha's mistress.' At the head of the table sat Jackson, and at the foot his head bookkeeper, or *locum tenens*, Mr Thomas James Randel Sparks. Sparks was by birth an Englishman, about 30 years of age, well proportioned, and would have been goodlooking had it not been for his queer grey eyes, which were so remarkable as to earn for him, from the negroes, who are very happy at nicknames, the sobriquet of 'Glass Eye'. Like many who moved in wider hemispheres, he had experienced in his day, something of the volatility of that fickle dame,

Fortune having been twice exalted to the dignity of overseer, and as frequently fallen back to the rank of bookkeeper. Sparks himself maintained that all his misfortunes were owing to an 'inherent goodness of heart' which disqualified him for the office of negro-driver; but there were others, who with every good wish to 'Mass Tom', attributed his retrograde motions entirely to the rum bottle; and we are sadly afraid, as Mr Sparks must figure on our pages, that some of our readers will be induced to believe that this was not a matter of speculative opinion, but that facts had some hand in the scandal raised against the head bookkeeper. Breakfast consisted of salt herrings, roasted and boiled, which Busha cut in halves and shared out, occasionally asking 'roast or boiled?' 'head or tail?'. There were several kinds of roasted vegetables, good fresh butter and excellent coffee. Several questions were asked by Jackson and answered by Sparks. Nothing, however, attracted Vernon's attention except the announcement that 'Andrew had been found,' and 'Trial drenched with herring pickle'. The cruelty of pouring 'pickle' down a human creature's throat, was forgotten as he thought of the horrid lash that seemed now to hang over Andrew's back; for as he had been found, it was only reasonable to infer that antecedently he had been lost, and it was fearfully plain that Andrew had lost himself intentionally; in other words, had run away. However, from certain remarks which followed, it appeared that 'Trial' was a sick steer, and 'Andrew' a stray mule.

Breakfast having been summarily despatched, Vernon was directed to visit the grass cutters, the second and third gangs, see that the hogs received their quantum of boiled corn and actually eat it, that the cattle were watered, and their sores dressed. By the time these responsible duties were performed and the ducks and fowls (or the dukes and fools, as Jackson called them) counted, the shell blew, calling alike free-man and slave to dinner.

On the new bookkeeper's reaching the works, he perceived a group of negroes assembled at the stairs of the overseer's house, and the loud crack of the whip announced that the daily routine of flogging had commenced. The culprit, partially stripped, was stretched on the ground and held in that position by four men, and a driver placed on either side, their lashes fell alternately. Several punished on this occasion were women. As one of these was likely ere long to be a mother, she was considerately accommodated with a hole which was dug in the ground over which she was stretched. Some of these punished were accused of insubordination to the drivers; the others of laziness – a crime all but capital on estates.

At dinner the overseer and his bookkeepers were joined by the Millwright, George Waldy, whom Vernon soon discovered was one of the speakers accidentally overheard the preceding night. He seated himself opposite Vernon, looked at Jackson with his small blue eyes half closed and exclaimed, 'You d-d mean Scotchman, you placed that girl in the stocks again as soon as my back was turned.'

'I'll report yer insolence to the Attorney, sir, as soon as I see him, and learn if you are to dictate to me in the management of the estate,' returned Jackson, continuing to ladle out the soup.

'If you had the pluck of a dunghill cock,' returned Waldy, 'you'd throw off your coat and do for yourself, instead of running off like a school boy to complain to his master.' To this Jackson made no reply; and the millwright, not having been invited to partake of any of the good cheer that lay before him, very coolly helped himself from the nearest dish, and catching at the decanter as it performed its evolutions round the table, washed down his dinner with a very liberal portion of strong grog. Jackson, evidently with the design of appearing at ease, enquired of Vernon if he liked the country.[3]

'The climate is much milder,' replied Vernon, 'than I was led to expect, and the natural beauties of the country enchanting, but I hold the system of slavery in abhorrence; judging of it as spread before me by observation, I do not for a moment hesitate to pronounce it a disgrace to any country.'

'I thought much worse of slavery once, Mr Vernon, than I do now – and when ye ken as much of the negro character as I do, maybe ye'll allow that they are fit for nothing but slaves.'

'Slavery has made the negro what he is; he is crushed beneath its overpowering weight, and it is impossible to form any fair estimate of his moral powers where there is no room for their development.'

'Ye'll think differently when ye've had a little more dealings with them, Mr Vernon,' replied Jackson.

'I do not think that at all likely,' replied Vernon; 'it is quite possible that I may discover the propensities of slave to be more vicious than I am led to suppose from my present superficial knowledge, but that will not alter my premises that slavery has made the negro what he is – but rather strengthen my objection to slavery, since I discover that men that are slaves are more reprobate than others, other things being equal.'

'Bravo!' exclaimed Waldy. 'I agree with you young man. Allow me to enquire, Mr Vernon, if you come from the Thames or the Tweed?'

'From the Thames,' replied Vernon with a smile and a slight inclination of the head.

'I thank God,' said Waldy, 'I am a fish of that river. Slavery is a curse and a disgrace to humanity, and it's certain that those who began the traffic in flesh and blood are now slaves in hell.' He then drank up the remainder of his grog, threw back his chair abruptly and stalked out of the room.

The overseer, who seemed now to breathe freely endeavoured to solicit the views of Sparks on the slavery question, but that gentleman's taciturnity on every subject likely in any way to interfere with his 'restoration to office' prevented his offering more than an ambiguous reply to any of the questions propounded either by Jackson or Vernon. Had the manifested sympathy for the sentiment [been] expressed by the latter, he might have been scouted as a renegade to the planting interests, yet as he had forcible reasons for cultivating the goodwill of the antislavery bookkeeper, he would not fairly come out on the side of the former, his most favourable position seemed to be a doubtful neutrality. Time rolled on heavily-yet it did roll on and Vernon became more and more accustomed to hard fare and unhappy faces; he had become quite a favourite among the negroes, and 'Father Williams,' the old Baptist leader, declared publicly in the crop house[4] that 'Massa above, had sent him in marcy to help de sufferers in dere captivity' and that though Vernon was 'a white man, he had a black heart.'

TWO₅

*I*t was Friday evening and the delinquents, as usual, were brought forward to receive the brutal punishment by the lash. There was unusual excitement. Vernon was there, and was, evidently, the ringleader of the tumult, which had been produced by Mary Ann Peach having been brought from the stocks to be flogged. This girl was the daughter of a former overseer, and had never before been subjected to the ordeal of the driver's lash. Cruel as the punishment was, girls of her caste dreaded it less than the indignity of being partially stripped in the public millyard. Her mother stood by her side weeping bitterly; Jackson was at his usual post, Vernon, was near him and in earnest conversation. From their position what passed could not be heard by those below, yet all knew he pleaded for Mary Ann. A little in the rear stood Miss Brown, and tears were on her cheeks. Jackson was inexorable; and Vernon, at his wits' end. [He] thought of a rescue, but saw it was impracticable: there was none to aid, hope seemed at an end, the last woman from the field-gang screamed and writhed beneath the lash. Mary Ann's turn came next, and her mother, half frantic, to solicit the overseer's clemency, fell on her knees. Loud murmurings were heard, the driver paused, the overseer, with an oath, reiterated his order. There was a buzz and then a shout and the attorney drove up the gate. Vernon flew to the carriage, and was so cordially greeted by the old gentleman that the negroes were convinced of what they before suspected, that Vernon was not an ordinary bookkeeper. The trustee immediately ordered Mary Ann to be released. The old woman threw herself at his feet and in her simple way poured forth her gratitude; she was a well tried and confidential domestic, and had been placed in care of the Great-House, a place of trust, as a reward for past services. Mr Fleming said something kindly to her and passed into the house. Meanwhile Mary Ann had grasped Vernon's hand and bathed it with tears of gratitude.

On reaching the hall where Jackson was, Mr Fleming said angrily: 'I told you before, Mr Jackson, that you were not to lay the brown girls down and whip them in the public yard. If the house girls are to be punished it must be in some other way.'

'Nothing, sir,' replied Jackson, 'will take the impertinence out of that girl but the whip. I have put her frequently into the stocks, and kept her there for a week at a time, but she comes out as saucy and impertinent as she went in.'

'And pray, sir,' asked Mr Fleming, 'what crime had the girl been guilty of to render it necessary to subject her to the punishment of the whip?' 'Impertinence and disobedience of order in leaving the property at night,' replied Jackson.

'Mary Ann waited on me for about three years, and I seldom had occasion to find any fault with her, if she is at her post during the day I don't see that it concerns you where she spends the night,' replied the Attorney. Mary Ann now entered the hall and curtseying said, 'Beg Trustee parden. But me blige to peak, in me own right. Busha tell me same mus lef Missus Waldy so cum lib we im, but me sa no, me couldn't do no such a ting. Since I been a little gal I been lib we Mass George, an im neber mek I want for nutin, an im buy mi from Mammy fare [?] out. Case me sa me wunt lef Mass George dat mek Busha parsecute me all time, look yar trustee, no see how stocks cut me foot'; Here Mary Ann put forward one of her feet on which the Iron Shackle had left some remarkable scars. 'Busha tell im ober an ober agen a wunt'; and the girl folded her arms across her breasts, cut her eyes at the crest-fallen Busha and looked the picture of injured innocence.[6] Mary Ann now thought this an excellent opportunity for setting forth her grievances, and, entering the house, she stood at the door and curtseying, laid such charges against the 'Busha' as awakened in the tender heart of Catherine Brown (who overheard all) some very painful and jarring feelings. Her conjugal rights suddenly seemed in danger of being invaded, and she was surprised and annoyed to find how very nearly love and murder were allied to each other, as illustrated in the drama about to be played out by her faithless swain and Mary Ann. The Attorney listened with considerable patience to these statements; and the girl, having at length concluded, crossed her hands, 'cut her eye' at the crest-fallen overseer, and looked at the picture of 'injured innocence'– her virtue had caused all her trouble.[7]

The 'Busha's Mistress' who now had her eyes opened by Mary Ann's story, stood forth with all the rage of a jealous and indignant woman. Jackson quailed beneath the flash of her eye.

'Oh, then,' she exclaimed, 'the truth has come out, and I jus' see what you wanted with this woman, Mr Jackson; and my mind is quite make up. You shan't make convenience of me; and trustee,' addressing Mr Fleming, she said, 'can the Busha mek I live with him 'ga'nst me wishes?'

'Come, come, Catherine, you are getting as bad as the other one now,' said the old gentleman; 'I thought you were sensible. Well' he said, coaxingly, laying his hand on her shoulder: 'When you have made up your mind to leave this gentleman let me know.'[8] Then turning to Jackson he continued: 'It appears to me that you are a kind of joint stock property – one claims your heart, and the other your body.'

'And, trustee,' continued Catherine, pursuing her inquiries, 'ain't I to get me days, as well as all them 'tother? For this year gone I never gets single day; as for church, I can't tell the last time I ever see the inside of a church.'

'Why Catherine, you must remember when you went to be christened; that is only ten years ago, and I suppose you will go again, when you are to be married,' said Mr Fleming. Then, facing Jackson, he continued: 'Mind you don't attempt to punish Mary Ann in this way again. Now I will give Catherine a drink of rum,[9] it will soothe her. He did so, but it would appear that the 'soothing syrup' administered by the Attorney produced only a momentary effect on the irritability under which she laboured. Mary Ann was quite satisfied with the happy turn things had taken, as far as her interests were concerned, and especially happy at the opportunity afforded of making her defence in *propria persona* before one so learned in all the manners and customs of the slaves as was Mr Fleming.

Jackson during this scene had sat at a window looking out, striving with all his might to attain something that would look like composure. On the women's leaving the hall he rose as the Attorney approached, who having leisurely taken a seat recapitulated succinctly the various circumstances in his management of the estate that had recently produced great dissatisfaction among the slaves. He distinctly stated that he was determined that no tyranny should be permitted on any property under his care, nor should any negro be punished to gratify private pique; and he hinted in pretty broad terms to Jackson that the next squabble of the kind that occurred would mean his instant dismissal. Then Mr Fleming proceeded to the Great House, and the overseer to the fields, where he vented his spleen in several petty ways on the two drivers, swearing (to what no one who heard him doubted) that they were the biggest rascals on the property. During the evening, however, he made several vain attempts to drive the thoughts of what had recently transpired from his mind. He knew the violence of Catherine's jealousy; he had once before smarted too painfully from its effects to forget it. Whilst all ran smoothly he was ignorant of the strength of his attachment to this woman; but now that she expressed her determination to leave him, it pressed painfully on his mind. He called to remembrance the attentions which Catherine had always paid to Vernon and the high opinions she had frequently passed in his favour. The recollection, too, that those feelings seemed quite reciprocal (of which a handsome shawl and other trifling presents presented and accepted, were substantial proofs) diminished in no degree the fears that were lurking in Jackson's breast. True, as men, women, and children had been recipients of Vernon's presents, little or nothing need have been thought of it; but now that the green-eyed monster reared his head, molehills became mountains.

On his return to the house, Jackson found Catherine dressed and ready to take her departure, having sent her box and child on before, to her aunt Downey, who was one of the satellites of the great house. We will not go so far as to assert that Catherine had intentionally delayed her departure. It certainly was not her fault that her hair would not curl as gracefully as she thought it ought to do; she said the macassar oil was bad and that the man who sold it was a rogue. Besides, her fancy boots could not be got on without a great deal of trouble (though a silver spoon had been substituted for a shoe horn and used with spirit and perseverance) because 'the girl that bought them was a fool'; and then Mary Ann came in for her share, and she called her something worse than either rogue or fool. Poor Catherine, she really was in a sad anti-Christian spirit. But many things that are slow in progression do come to an end at last. So it was with Catherine's toilet, and at last she put her shawl around her shoulders – yes, the very shawl Vernon had given her; the very article that the greeneyed fiend had been holding before Jackson's eyes as his mule carried him slowly through the intervals of the cane fields, the whole evening. He couldn't be mistaken in the article, it was of silk cotton with a deep silk fringe. This Catherine now in spread over her shoulders in graceful folds; and as she admired both it and herself in the glass, she fastened it in front with a gold brooch, and again she turned to the glass and there she removed the pin further up – and then she stuck it a little lower down, and said it would do very well. After this she opened a band-box [?] and tied on a tuscan hat, trimmed with very broad and very bright ribbon. When she saw Jackson coming she was just ready. He tried to coax her to remain, but without effect; and then he snatched off her shawl and trampled it under his feet, but Catherine picked it up and replaced it on her shoulders. He had broken the pin of her brooch, she said, but that she didn't mind; but she was glad he had not torn her shawl, for she thought a great deal of it and would not have it injured for worlds. Then before he could speak, she brushed past him and was gone. She had the cards in her hands, and it was her turn to deal them out. Cleopatra might have triumphed as completely over Caesar as she had over Anthony had she known where he was vulnerable. Leaving Catherine, however, for the present to pursue her way to 'Aunt Downey's', we shall see what has become of Mary Ann.

Having left the overseer's house, she marched directly to the kitchen, where she was welcomed by Phoebe the cook, who was pounding coffee in a wooden mortar and expatiating with Ben and Eliza on her hairbreadth escape.

'True,' said the washerwoman, 'if Massa Vernon no been keep back Busha, Mary Ann would a flog done 'fore Trustee 'rive; hi, de bokra, sah, hab good heart. Hi! to tink 'pon a gal like Mary Ann, who hab white pussin fe im revelations to be trip and flog in de publik yard! Hi! true wa' minister say tadder day – man is like de grass a de fele', an me don't tink woman is much better.'

'Dar so, cousin,' replied the cook.[10]

'Cousin, Mary Ann,' said Phoebe, 'you can't 'peak tell we say wanah Trustee and Busha da say to you and Miss Brown in ar house?'

'Hi,' replied Mary Ann, 'you tink say Busha dare fe open 'im mout' to Trustee; but me 'peak up well, ar sure you, an' tell Trustee de hole 'tory, an mi possecute im tell Busha say and him won hab no sich going on; dat if me tan' to me bisness durance de day, 'im don't see de cashun im mus interferance wid me durance de night.'

'Den you will able go dar Maxfield go see Mr Waldy when you pleasin to do so,' said the cook.

'Dar so cousin,' answered Mary Ann; 'long as me ten' to me ployment dar day-time, An' Miss Brown, him is going to lef Busha; Trustee as good as say Mr Jackson can't hindrance im. But, you no' cousin, war me da tink pon, dar Misser Vernon, if e no bin fe im, hi, da would been ar disgrace ar would ar come to? To flog 'fore all dem black negar in a yard, trip an' disposed!'

There was also a confabulation in the bookkeeper's barracks between Vernon and Sparks.

'Have you found out yet,' enquired Sparks of Vernon, 'who that pretty girl is that always lives with Mrs Christy?'[11]

Vernon's cheek crimsoned for a moment, but the next instant the colour disappeared, and he replied: 'She is Mrs Christy's niece, I believe.'

'Just as much as she is mine; she was born at the Great House, that I know; and I strongly suspect has a daub of the tar-bush in her composition,' said Sparks.

'What does that mean in plain English?' enquired Vernon, endeavouring to appear unconcerned, yet betraying his surprise.

'That she has a taint of African blood.' replied Sparks.

'Oh! you are quite figurative; you mean to insinuate that one or other of her parents was coloured,' said Vernon.

'Her mother was, I suppose,' answered Sparks.

'Who was her mother?' enquired Vernon.

'You had better ask old Fuller that,' replied Sparks.

'What does he know about the matter?', said Vernon.

'More than he dares tell,' answered Sparks.

'Her mother – what became of her? You said Miss Celeste was born here?' replied the new bookkeeper.

'Why, that's her tomb, under the large promgranate, so the old man says. I am sure, though, that her relatives were respectable, judging by the slab on the tomb.'

'Why so? The poorest slaves try to place a tombstone over their relatives' graves,' said Vernon.

'Yes, but slaves don't deal in marble slabs,' replied Sparks.

'I always thought the young lady was Mrs Christy's niece,' said Vernon.

'So did I, until old Fuller let the cat jump out of the bag.'

Here the head bookkeeper was summoned by the cattleman who had been waiting for some time at the foot of the stairs for sheep-wash and fish oil to dress certain wounds inflicted on 'Eve' by 'Peter,' the beef boy, during his ride to the stall on the previous day – for which crime the said Peter was then doing penance in the stocks. Having snatched at a huge bunch of rusty padlock keys, which Vernon designated his 'seals of office', Sparks, taking care to doff his Sunday coat and sable neckkerchief, which had been assumed to grace the dining table, adjourned the committee of scrutiny to attend to matters which more legitimately claimed his attention.

For some little time after Catherine's departure from the overseer's domicile, things were managed in the culinary department of the establishment tolerably well. Then there was a sad falling off. At breakfast the coffee was wretched and muddy, the vegetables burnt on one morning and practically raw on another, and when, as usual, the bookkeepers chose 'roast or boiled,' 'head or tail,' it [the herrings], was so intolerably salt as to be unpalatable. At dinner the soup, whether pepper-pot or pease, was unsavoury, and evinced a great want of taste and the viands were either over or under done. Phoebe had been flogged twice, and very severely indeed, yet matters were not mended; no they were not – the eye, the nose, the palate, each said they were not. The house, too, soon lost its neat and tidy appearance. Everything was by sixes and sevens; nothing looked cozy. Tubs of dirty water and orange peel that had been used in cleaning the rooms, stood on the staircase or in the portico; the floor had lost its polish and swarms of flies covered the entry table, on which were ranged glasses containing slops or cups and saucers with dregs. The house girls had been placed in the stocks, kicked, cuffed, and cursed; but still there was no visible improvement in household affairs; they were nothing bettered, but rather grew worse.

Jackson himself was as much out of sorts as his establishment, and grumbled, cursed, or swore perpetually. He shot one of his dogs and drowned both the cats, knocked Mary Ann down with the knife case and one of the house girls with a candlestick, spoke pettishly to everyone, and swore he would discharge Sparks the next time he got drunk, and was frosty even to strangers when they called. For awhile he remained mewed up in the house. With his legs cocked up against the window, he looked down far away over the sloping ground at the wide ocean stretching out from the bay of Salt Marsh. Now and then he would take the glass from over the door where it hung, and mark the progress of some vessel as it passed along majestically on the surface of the mighty deep. True it mattered not to him whether ship or brig; nor did he care whither it was bound, but he did this because he had been accustomed to do it before; and then he would replace the glass and resume his seat – and Catherine would be uppermost in his mind. He would wonder whether she was at her aunt's or at some of her friends, whether nursing her baby or at her needlework; if she had curled her hair, or placed it as she sometimes did, behind her ears; and would have liked to have known whether she had taken off the rings he gave her, as she did when they quarrelled before; and he thought he saw her before him with the shawl and tuscan bonnet. Then the ideal of Catherine would vanish from his mind for a while and his thoughts would stray unbidden to 'Caledonia stern and wild' and to many faces and scenes passed forever. He thought of his mother, his sister Lucy, and Molly Parker, the Miller's daughter, whom he used to love and call sweetheart when they met alone at the turnpike near Widow Vaunes's cottage, and he'd half make up his mind to return to his native land and marry Molly and live with his mother, and read his Bible, go to the Kirk and be happy. Then something would disturb his reverie and he would walk out, mount his mule, ride off to the fields and think of other days and other things.

On Sunday evening after dark Jackson bent his steps towards the Great House. He was undecided as to his movements, whether he would go to the house where Catherine was, or merely call to bid Mrs Christy good evening. As he drew near he recognised Catherine's melodious voice. She was singing one of those plaintive ditties so common among the uneducated. Jackson's steps led him mechanically to the house. He listened for a while and then tapped gently at the door and said in a low tone, 'Catherine!'

'You is mistaken the house, Mr Jackson,' replied Catherine; 'it isn't Catherine you want, 'tis Mary-Ann, an' she is [not here].'[12] Her aunt, however, not daring to resent a visit from Busha, opened the door. The house in question[13] had been built for the domestic in care of the Great House, and stood at some little distance from that edifice. It was surrounded by a little garden that furnished herbs required in the culinary department, to which, indeed, Mary Downy most properly belonged, but as fires seldom now blazed in the old fashioned kitchen of the establishment, Mrs Downy's situation was quite a sinecure, as well as a post of honour. The cottage comprised two rooms and an entry; one of these was a bed chamber, the other a kind of parlour and contained the usual quantity of chairs and tables required for two or three persons besides a table above the ordinary dimensions, on which Mary Downy did her ironing when she assumed the character of laundress, which was about as often as Mrs Christie and her protege visited Greenside. There was also here articles for ornament as well as for use. In the lattice-worked shelf, just above the largest window, were all manner of plates, cups, saucers, and basins of many colours, on which were emblazoned kings, queens, ships of war, and large bunches of flowers. In one corner of the room stood a table and tray on which were placed tumblers and wine glasses, an old water jar with a broken spout, and a bright tin lamp in an old China saucer which now burnt brilliantly. The opposite angle contained a small cupboard through the glass door of which sundry flasks and bottles were seen, like prisoners looking through their grated windows. These bottles contained wine and spirits, lawful perquisites from the large establishment over which Mrs Downy presided; for no one ever hinted that the headhouse woman's claim to the remnants of the table, whether in the shape of liquids or solids, were not legitimate – not even the head bookkeeper who, frequently on Sunday evenings (when, as he said, 'he had nothing else in the world to do'), honoured the keeper of the Great House with a visit, when he not only saw these bottles, but tasted their contents. But as Mary Downy knew that it was beneath the dignity of a Busha to 'wet his whistle' in her house, the aforesaid receptacle of bottles was not opened on this occasion; she made no further advances than the offer of one of her best chairs from which, with her apron, she had brushed away every particle of dust. Catherine sat nearly in the centre of the room nursing her baby. Jackson drew near and took her hand, but she withdrew it abruptly.

'Won't you make friends Catherine,' he said, 'and come home?'

'Home!' she said. 'Home! Has a slave got any home? He is here today and there to-morrow; he is sent to work on any property that Trustee please and p'raps sold if massa or young massa owes money. Look at me sister Sarah! Me eber see him since de day marshal put de handcuff on him an drag 'im off de place; an didn't everybody say old Mr Hine was a rich man ? De grave is de home for such as we. An dis baby, I is wicked 'nough to wish sometimes it was dead, when I tink say what it is to come to if it live to grow up. Maybe say some drunkard Busha will kick it down de steps and break its back, like dat brute at Maxfield do Jimmy's little boy.'

'Well ,Catherine,' replied Jackson, 'if you behave well I will buy both you and the child from the estate.'

'I am behaved bad?' enquired Catherine, looking askance with a degree of contempt. 'You ever seen me brazen? It ain't to-day I hear the story talk of you buying me. 'Spose you'll buy me like Jack Mowatt buy Sally – buy im when he was please and sell im when he get tired of him – dat mek massa say he won't sell any of him people 'cept dem is to be free. If you can't even buy me, you can't buy de baby? If you get discharge 'spose I am to hand over to de new Busha whether I like him or hate him. See Nancy Lewes, what she is come to, a gal dat use to wear shoes and stockings when her father was 'live, an' could even read de newspaper! I don't tink Nancy can well tell who is de fardar of him two children. Toder-day me speak to him for her own good, an' she say, "Pig ax him mumma war mek him mout' long so; 'im mumma say, tan, pickney, tell you grow, you mout' will long so too."'

'What did she mean by that?' asked Jackson.

'She mean say,' replied Catherine, 'that once she was like me, and bumby I will stan' like she. I tell you de truth, Mr Jackson, I is intend to take Fader Williams' 'vice an' jine de Church.

Jackson having made several further attempts to coax her home, returned at length alone.

A few days after this there was an uproar at the overseer's house between Waldy and Jackson. The fracas occurred during dinner. The former dashed a tumbler of grog into the face of the latter, who returned the compliment by throwing a round of beef at his head. The missile, however, 'missed its man', and striking Sparks in the face, disfigured that gentleman's nose, and so completely threw his soup plate off its equilibrium as to pour its contents (which were boiling hot) into his lap. Waldy now aimed a blow at Jackson with his fist which felled him to the floor. Quick as the electric shock Catherine darted into the room and rushed between them. Her long dark hair was disheveled, her bright eyes flashed, and her whole frame was tremulous with emotion. In her hand she flourished a large carver. Eyeing Waldy with a look of defiance, she exclaimed: 'Touch him again if you dare, and I'll wash you in your blood.' Waldy fell back directly and was laid hold of by Vernon, while 'Glass-Eye', with a pretty fair sprinkling of blood and soup, stood forth by far the most ludicrous figure of the group. Waldy was led out by Vernon, Sparks followed; and Catherine, having discovered that Jackson was more frightened than hurt, hurried out to see after her infant which she had thrown aside in her precipitancy to arrive at the overseer's house as early as Waldy, for whom she had been on the lookout ever since she had learnt that he threatened Jackson.

Poor Mary Ann, who had gone down to the tank for water presently returned, in 'blissful ignorance' of all that had transpired during her brief absence and, having set down her pail in the pantry, as her ill stars would have it, walked with all humility into the hall where Busha, who had scarcely recovered from his perturbation, sat in a kind of brown study to ask for a pass, six days being now due as Ellen, whose days had transpired, was now returned to her pantry and plates. Her reception, as might have been anticipated by those acquainted with the recent hubbub that had damaged the head bookkeeper's nose and trouserloons, was rather frosty; for as Mary Ann attributed all her troubles to Busha, so did Busha accuse Mary Ann as the infernal – who had placed him, by her blabbing, in his present uneasy 'fix'. After an infinity of oaths and a volley of abuse, in which the name generally applied to the feminine of a lower animal species was very liberally sprinkled, and a threat to 'break her neck down the steps', she was ordered to Sparks for a pass, which he sincerely hoped would carry her to hell. Wondering at Busha's unexpected and virulent attack, she grumbled her way over to the barracks and, popping her head into 'Mass Tom's' room, she found him holding a large iron key to his eye and d-g the butcher for sending a round of beef with 'such a rascally large bone in it', and occasionally applying his finger and thumb to his nostrils to ascertain if the blood had entirely ceased to flow.

'Why-oh! Me massa get me!' exclaimed Mary Ann. 'Mass Tom, me good bakra, you can't done da fill you head wid spirit so? Rum will kill you, if you keep on da follow e so! My king! looker em trousers and shut; how e tan!'

Sparks, who would have borne this rebuke badly enough, had his predilection for the 'fire water' really conduced to his dilemma, having the greatest aversion to the most oblique reference being made to his habits of tippling, flew into a violent passion, sent the candlestick flying at her head and seemed to reciprocate fully the overseer's wish to consign Mary Ann to main quarters, for he told her to go to the devil. The girl, however, like many in more elevated positions, hesitated to obey an order so particularly disagreeable; and, instead of going where the overseer wished, and the bookkeeper ordered her, walked direct to the kitchen – which is decidedly, the very best place on an estate for hearing the news of the day, and entered into a friendly confabulation with the cook.

'Aunty,' said Mary Ann, 'war matter we Busha and Mass Tom?'

'Den,' answered the cook, 'You no been yerry say Cato carry de beef and run gone,' speaking of what was most uppermost in her thoughts perhaps.

'War' bout beef?' asked Mary Ann, with an air of surprise.

'War' bout beef?' said the cook, in a mocking tone; 'you is fool as a new negar; you no been a house when you ole man and Busha da fi tee out?'

'Mass Tom don't me ole man. Me no hab no ole man, 'cepin Mass George,' returned Mary Ann petulantly.

'Tis 'im a mean,' replied Phoebe, 'im no knock down Busha; Busha no trow de corn beef after him; corn beef no miss him so pyle [spoil] "Glass-Eye" face and trousers; Cato no catch up de beef run gone? Dat is a very imperance dog, a wish say 'tis him ben shoot place a prig.' The impudence of 'Cato' and her charitable wish in his behalf was said rather to herself.

'Den Mass George lef 'im 'ployment quite a Maxfield, come ober yah to fite me Busha. Po' me gal, me sorry say me eber drop the wod out a me mouth to tell him say Busha put me dar bilbo. True war negar say, "trouble day dar bush, Anancy bring e come a house"'; and she sat down on the mortar, placed her hand under her chin, and began to sob quite in earnest.

Waldy's physical powers having placed him beyond the vengeance of Jackson, and the attorney's injunctions in favour of Mary Ann being of rather too recent a date to be violated, he hit on an expedient, which promised a considerable degree of revenge. Trumping up some charge against Mary Ann's two brothers, he had them flogged very cruelly, and then brushed off with ebony (i.e., scourged with ebony birches after). They were then washed with herring pickle and consigned to the dungeon with the assurance that the medicine should be repeated as soon as the first dose had properly operated on the solids, and that they should be kept on very low diet, to prevent any possible excitement of the system. Vernon was not at home when this occurred; but on being informed of the barbarous act on his return, he determined without reference to consequences, to prevent, if possible, its repetition. The two Poachers he knew to be very well behaved lads, and their punishment, he was convinced, was only a colateral [sic] blow at their sister.

The estate dungeon was a prototype of the 'black hole of Calcutta'. Damp and dark as midnight; the air unwholesome, the effluvia arising from it intolerable. From one end of the vault to the other projected an iron bar on which were shackles to receive the feet: to this bar the culprits were fastened by one or both feet. Here it was the custom to confine those slaves that had been very severely whipped lest they should run away and expose themselves and thus excite, if nothing else, a degree of sympathy from some whose hearts had not yet reached the consistency of the 'nether millstone'. Besides, there were a few Justices of the Peace, with Mr Benjamin at their head (a gentleman of the Hebrew persuasion), who had evinced their meddling propensities so far 'with other persons' property', as to lay certain grave charges before the Colonial Minister. Now as this 'meddling' had led to the development of some circumstances which conduced to a rather lengthy correspondence between Custos Millar and the Colonial Office on one occasion; to save time and trouble it seemed best to prevent 'facts' which might, either in the hands of the Secretary for the Colonies or the anti-slavery party, become 'stubborn things', coming under the cognisance of this philanthropic clique.

The key of this tomb of the living seldom passed from the overseer's hands. The scanty supply of food allowed its inmates was passed through a hole made in the mossy wall in such a way as to admit air and exclude the light. At night a watchman was placed near to prevent escape or their friends ministering in any way to their comforts. The man selected for this duty was an African called Quamin, one of Busha's instruments of cruelty; he was held in abhorrence by his fellow slaves, as he performed the duties connected with the dungeon with alacrity and zeal worthy of a better cause. This of course raised him high in the favour of the overseer, and he was frequently rewarded for his efficient aid by a present of rum or an extra allowance. On the other hand, any derelection [sic] of duty subjected him to the tender mercies of the drivers. To carry out the preventive measures determined on by Vernon, two things were necessary – possession of the dungeon key and the removal of this man from his post. It is not unlikely that he might have been bribed, but as soon as the lash fell on him his secret would have bolted out, for Quamin was an infamous coward, as our next chapter will show.

Chapter

THREE

—— ∞ ——

The Midnight Adventure [14]

The night was dark and dismal; not a star was visible in the heavens. The bare outlines of a figure could be seen as it descended stealthily the stone staircase of the overseer's house. It was Catherine. As she emerged from the portal, the watchman at the works roared at the pitch of his voice, 'A-l-l-s well.' The next moment the cry was taken up by the cattle-pen watchman and then responded to by Quamin [15] at the dungeon. In a few minutes the echo died away, every murmur was hushed, and the silence of mid-night reigned.

Catherine was now met by Mary Ann and they proceeded to the bookkeeper's barracks. She tapped gently at Vernon's door and said in a whisper, 'I've got the key'. Vernon joined them immediately and they wended their way to the hospital. Under the arch of the staircase they drew up and Vernon rigged [up] a machine by means of which he hoped to get rid of the watchful African. He had procured a large calabash in which he cut holes to resemble eyes mouth and nose; through a hole in the bottom he introduced a lighted candle and placed a roll of brimstone in the aperture answering to the mouth. This he fastened with a cord to the top of two sticks put together in the shape of the letter T and spread a sheet over the cross. It then resembled a shrouded spectre. Lighting the brimstone, he stooped behind the figure and slowly approached the watchman's hut, dragging after him a piece of old iron chain. Quamin heard the tinkling and came out rubbing his half-sleepy eyes. He gave one look and a horrid scream, and with something between a hop, step and a jump, he cleared the stone-wall, rushed through a penguin fence, fell flat on his face, picked up himself in a trice, gave one look behind, saw the 'Duppy', smelt the brimstone, heard the chain, uttered another shriek of horror, and with a spring left the outer wall behind him. Nor did he venture once to look behind until he reached the negro houses, where he alarmed the inmates and told them that he had seen 'Cudjo's' ghost in the very shroud in which he had been buried; that brimstone flamed from his mouth, and fire from his eyes; that he had a great sword in one hand and a stick in the other, with which he had run after him and knocked him down; that he must have 'broke way' from a bad place as he had chains on his hands, feet and neck; and [he] concluded his frightful story by swearing (to what it was not likely any one would doubt) that if Busha killed him he would never watch 'ar dungeon agen'.

Having so effectually succeeded in scaring Quamin, Vernon returned to the girls and they proceeded to open the dungeon which, after some little trouble, they effected and the heavy door grated on its rusty hinges; the effluvia drove them back, and it was some minutes before they recovered from the sickening blast of the dungeon simoon. Having liberated the men and furnished them with some money and clothes, which had been brought by their sister, they were hurried away and urged to hasten on as fast as possible, lest they should be overtaken by their overseers in the morning. Leaving the dungeon door open the party then hurriedly retraced their steps to the works. Catherine found Jackson still fast asleep and returned the key to his pocket; he had been 'keeping it up' with a few of his boon and bottle companions, aided by Sparks, who had been invited to take part in the spree as a kind of 'peace offering' for the spoilation of his olfactory organ by the unhappy round of bee[f]. Of these movements Catherine was apprised and knew it was her opportunity; she had been the cause of the punishment barbarously inflicted on the two men and she thought it her duty to run any risk to save them from a repetition. The news of the horrid 'Duppy' that Quamin had seen at the dungeon spread like wild-fire through the estate. In the field during breakfast time, whispering knots with grave faces and uplifted eyes were seen in every direction, and everybody wished to see somebody that had heard the story from Quamin's own lips. The drivers felt half inclined to throw down their whips and join the gang, and those whose turn it was to watch at the cattle-pen and at the works that night were calculating their chances of giving leg-ball;[16] some of the gang even dared to insinuate that Mr Vernon, a white man, who wasn't afraid of the trustee or even of Busha 'self, was quite 'timorous', for they had heard him say he should ask Sparks to go with him at night to call the watch. But the field-gang were not the only enquirers and calculators of this momentous subject.

The members of the kitchen, as soon as a quorum had been formed in the meeting, entered into a description of this 'ghostly' question. Quamin, following his prisoners, passed through Maxfield at an early hour and called up, as a matter of course, and gave a very elaborate account of the event in which he had cut so prominent a figure; and Jane White (one of the house-girls who happened then to be on a kind of three days parole of honour, inasmuch as she was at liberty to go to the world's-end could she manage to return therefrom before the expiration of three days due her for attention to the pantry when she ought to have been at church) was sent over to Greenside to learn full particulars, as the reports that had reached the domestics on that estate, through a boy, who had the story from his mother, who heard it from a watchman, was vague and very unsatisfactory.

Jenny, knowing that the cook would be in possession of full particulars, walked directly to the kitchen and having received and duly returned the usual morning salutation of 'morrah', without waiting to be asked took her seat on the mortar which, except when in use, was always placed on its side as a kind of kitchen 'woolsack'. Phoebe, who was just then engaged in passing her fingers through her little boy 'Nickky's' head in search perhaps of phrenological lumps, ever and anon bringing her thumb nails together and turning the vegetables that were roasting for breakfast, at first blush evinced no inclination for a confab. The ambassador from Maxfield, however, seemed determined to solicit an elucidation and began by the following enquiry:

'True, Aunty, me yerry say Quamin been see rowling calf a de dungeon las' night, wi' chain and fire and brimstone 'pon 'im.'

'A true fe sartin,' answered Phoebe; 'Quamin no wake we las' night jis second cock-crow. It no to say duppy so-so, but duppy and rowlin' calf all mix up. Him hab horn, im carry chain oh! 'im carry sword oh! an junka 'tick an pistol, brimstone, gunpowder, fi re, all come out a him mout'; him most pull ebry bit a de hare out a Quamin head and knock 'im down we' 'im big stick, and tan ober him wi' 'im sword. Hi! Po' me gal, warrah dey come to de wul? Me yerry say Farder Williams' ten' to 'splain de fac' out a de wud to-night yah.'[17]

The excitement of the 'ghost' diminished with the passing of the days, for it was soon forgotten. Jackson's spirits fell lower and lower, and one afternoon he invited over Dr Wagstaff, the local practitioner, along with Mr Granger, Jock Mowatt and Fidler of the neighbouring estate for a 'good old spree'. The party supped well and drank better. After they had fully regaled themselves some were inclined to sleep and some to joke. The liquor was laid out. Granger took a favourable opportunity to throw something into one of the decanters on the side board. As the decanter was of blue glass the difference in colour could not be perceived.

On the brandy being served round, Doctor Wagstaff leisurely opened his eyes and asked, as he had done before:

'What's the matter?'

'Brandy, Doctor; will you join us with a glass?' said Jackson.

'I don't mind if I do,' replied Dr Wagstaff. The Doctor took a pretty good bitch and smacking his lips, said 'it was the thing itself.'

Fidler held it to be genuine cognac, whilst Granger rather rudely declared that had his mother given him such milk, he'd be sucking still.

'Just a little drop, Doctor,' said Jackson, 'that I've by me in case of sickness. Ye ken, doctor, that its handy at times.'

'I am quite aware, Mr Jackson of the merits of brandy as a medicine,' replied Dr Wagstaff. 'I think it kills as often as it cures; it's quite a popular kind of physic among the planters, Mr Jackson, any how; ha! ha! ha!'

The doctor was just about once more to compose himself in order to finish his afternoon's nap, when his eyes fell on the box of cigars, whereon he 'hemmed' once or twice, adjusted his cravat, and enquired if they were genuine Havanahs.

'Spects they are, doctor,' said Granger.

'Try one, doctor,' said Fidler; 'I know you're a capital judge.'

'Don't mind if I do, gentlemen,' said Dr Wagstaff drawing up and selecting a well wrapped one from the box.

'I dare say,' said Granger, 'those checks of Manhead's against the bank are still out.'

'I haven't any of them in my locker,' said Jock Mowatt.

'I am athinking Jock, 'tis d-d few of any checks lying on your hands,' said Granger.

'The more's the shame to me after twenty years' hard work,' replied Jock.

Here the doctor began to overhaul his old leather pocket book, but found nothing save his friend Bonkvah's IOU for two pounds ten, and his butcher's bill which, though long overdue, was still minus a receipt. He, however, looked very profound and said:

'I am glad, Mr Jackson, I've been rid of all Mr Manhead's paper; some time ago I held a good round sum in his checks.'

'You're quite lucky, doctor,' said Fidler.

'How many hogsheads, last week, Jock?' enquired Granger.

'Eight,' replied Jackson, 'grinding d—d old rations all the week, stopped fire half the time.'

'Stop't fire?' said Granger.

'Whenever they stop fire with me, I makes pint of flogging every rascally neger at the works, and the boatswain in the bargain.'

'They can't help that,' said Jackson. 'You'll grind to eternity and not get a cyphon of liquor out of those old ratoons.'

'Help it or not, I always lick 'em, it makes 'em smart you see. Besides, if they don't deserve it for that, they're sure to deserve it for something else and all winds up with a good crop. That's just my way, and I've never made a bad crop this ten years,' said Granger.

'Its dry weather,' said Mowatt, holding up his glass.

'What'll ye have, gentlemen?' enquired Jackson.

'A long pull to be sure,' answered Mowatt, puffi ng the smoke from his mouth; 'these cigars make a fellow dry.'

'By George, Jackson,' said Granger, 'your grog must be old, getting rather sourish: taste it, Fidler, and try how you like it.'

'True as you say,' said Fidler; 'must be very old stuff indeed.'

'Bless my stars,' exclaimed Jackson, who had taken two or three mouthfuls, 'what the devil is the matter with the rum?'

'Must be rale old stuff,' said Granger, winking to the others with the corner of his eye.

'The same rum we've been drinking all dinner,' said Jackson. He now poured a little into a wine glass and on tasting it looked so completely bewildered as to overact the gravity of the party.

'It's that d—d rascal Granger,' said Jackson; 'he's always at his blackguard tricks; he has put vinegar into the rum.'

'Must be Jock,' said Granger; 'he carries such a grum, ugly face that he sours everything, wherever he goes. T'other day he just came into the boiling house and a whole cyphon of liquor got quite sourish.'

'You deserve to be drowned in a horsepond, Mr Granger,' said Jackson.

'You can't drown him,' returned Mowatt, 'because 'tis clear he's born to be hung, and those born to be hung will never be drowned.'

Here the company was a little interrupted by Dr Wagstaff's preparatory movements for emigrating. After considerable shuffling among the chairs in search for his spurs and whip, the sapient practitioner bade good evening, not, however, without prescribing for himself another dose of the only kind of medicine he seemed more willing to take than to prescribe.

Drinking and smoking was instituted until a late hour. Jock Mowatt got drunk and sang loud and long while Granger, who was in a similar plight, preferred having a fight – with whom, was a matter of no consequence. Several challenges having been politely declined, he at length fell fast asleep in his chair, on which Jock and Fidler, having previously shaved the huge whiskers from one side of his face, put him to bed and, removing the looking glass from his room, rode off to spend the night together, it not being deemed prudent to leave Mowatt to take care of himself.

Chapter

FOUR[18]

*D*uring crop time Vernon's post as second bookkeeper was the boiling house, while Sparks maintained the more responsible position of distiller. His chance of promotion seemed by a kind of fatality to be linked with alcohol; the more he made and less he drank the greater were his chances in the ascending scale. Truth, however, compels us to add that he failed sadly in one of these requirements, as the pimples on his face, denominated 'grog blossoms', together with the irritable state of his stomach in the morning would have been sufficient of themselves to prove, had he not more than once been found by his brother-bookkeeper under the stokehole nicely covered with trash enjoying a comfortable nap, this retreat having been provided for him by the slaves as they said 'to hide im way from Busha'.

Ill-health having obliged Vernon to relinquish his position on Greenside for awhile, the attorney took him down to the town of Falmouth for the benefit of sea-bathing and change of air. Having received a cordial invitation from a merchant to spend a few weeks in his family, he had an opportunity of witnessing some very remarkable freaks which were played off at the expense of the domestic slaves by his entertainer's wife, who certainly was an excellent model of a modern 'Xantipe'. Mrs Foster, or, as she was generally called by her neighbours, 'Madam Fungus', in person resembled a fillet of veal in petticoats; she was 'fat, fair, and forty'. Her cheeks were rather of the reguse order, and were only exceeded in their ruby tint by the hue of her locks. But if Mrs Foster's personal appearance defies the pen of the ready writer, surely her 'oddity' confounds 'all languages and things'. Priding herself on her household management,[19] she bustled from one part of her establishment to the other, promising much, performing little. Whoever enjoyed repose she determined that neither herself, husband or servants should be of the number. To her household she was a living pest, a walking plague, a sweeping fury. Nor were her neighbours exempt from her omniferous annoyances. It would be impossible to do anything like justice to the scenes she enacted without relating a few of the freaks as they occurred; but without the pencil of a Cruikshank it is impossible that anything of the spirit of her farces can be portrayed on paper.

Among her slaves there was a man whom she called 'Bruin', who was alternately butler, cook, or groom. This man she sometimes had tied and flogged, as she was much amused, she said, at the peculiar way the fellow had of bellowing. At certain times she would have him dressed up in a suit of regimentals and, placing an old musket in his hands, insist on her husband's putting him through manual and platform exercises. Sometimes he would be kept 'under arms' for half the day, or perhaps at mid-day ordered to bed.

A lady once on a visit to her house was much scandalized at seeing a young lad usurping the privileges of chamber-maid. At length she expressed her surprise.

'Oh! my dear,' replied Mrs Foster, 'it's only our girl Nancy; the wretch has broken some crockery and I've cropped her hair and rigged her up in a suit of Mr F's old clothes.'

One of her boys having cooked some steaks badly, she ordered him up to the dining hall, seated him at the head of the table, with one of her most fashionable dress caps on his head, placed half a dozen servants around him and stood by herself with a horsewhip until he had eaten every mouthful from the dish. It may be worth while to add that during these freaks she conducted herself with all the dignity of a Duchess, dressed perhaps in the most grotesque manner imaginable for, as regards her toilet, she certainly was a queen over all the daughters of pride. But, perhaps, one of her most humourous feats was the following, performed for the purpose of annoying her neighbours who had interfered a little with her movements:

Having had Bruin tied up and whipped very cruelly, it got rumoured that he was in danger of dying from the severity of the punishment. Foreseeing that this story might be turned to some account against her neighbours, she caused it to be whispered around that 'Bruin' certainly was in a very critical state. At length some of her own slaves (who were in the secret) reported that Bruin was dying and finally that he was dead. Now among several other duties, done and performed by Mr Foster, was that of adjusting the parochial weights and measures. (Charity would induce the hope that he adjusted these more correctly than he did the conduct of his rib.) These duties occasionally carried him to the utmost limits of the parish. Mr Foster being about to set out in the performance of this, if not lucrative, at least respectable, business had a long chest in which were the weights and measures by which those current were to be tested and placed in a cart. This his wife covered with a tarpauline as if it was desirable to secrete what was beneath. As it had been reported far and near by the servants that Bruin's corpse would be carried out of the town for interment at midnight, and one of the men had been seen to pass in and out with a spade and pickaxe, the neighbours remained on the watch, anxious for something to confirm all they had heard and seen, and were on the tip-toe of expectation when, at midnight, that cart was drawn out the yard and presently after the long black box moved slowly through the gate, the night guard was now sent for and the servant forbidden to stir an inch; every window was thrown open and many who had always fought shy and pretended that Mrs Foster and her concerns were beneath their notice, openly committed themselves. The constables, with a mob at their heels, soon made their appearance nearly out of breath and enquired where the murder had been committed. Soon the whole neighbourhood was in an uproar and a seizure and search were made in the 'King's name'. Mrs Foster now threw up her window, laughed heartily at the ladies who were posted at the opposite windows and indignantly ordered 'Bruin' to enquire why she was disturbed at such an unseasonable hour and to ascertain if any of the flock of white geese who lived round her had been frightened, as she heard a cackling in some of the houses. 'Bruin' was out instantly, laughing louder than the best of them could talk, to the chagrin of all in any way concerned in the affair. The constables immediately turned tail and the crowd dispersed, some shouting and laughing at the meddling neighbours, while others abused them for prying and peeping into other people's concerns and neglecting their own.

While in Falmouth Vernon had several opportunities of attending public sales of slaves levied on for taxes by the collecting constable, or for private judgements by the Deputy Marshal. Sometimes, too, families leaving the island would sell their slaves at auction.

The first sale of this kind was that of fourteen slaves, men, women and children of different ages and colour. No regard was paid to kindred ties, except when the child was of so tender an age as to require a parent's care; in such a case, mother and child always went together. Beyond this no enquiry was made. The slaves bore their separation with wonderful fortitude, or, rather, stoical apathy – with a solitary exception. There was one woman weeping and complaining bitterly of being now separated entirely from her only child who had been carried into another parish as a servant maid by one of the ladies of her master's family who, for some reason or other, had split off from the parent stock. Her husband, a middle aged black man, whose talents as a cooper had been highly extolled by the auctioneer, was standing by talking to her in a coaxing tone, but the noise made by the cryer, bidders and others who were laughing and talking very loudly, prevented what he said being overheard. However, as the men and women were sold in separate lots, the presumption was that the consolation she was now receiving, slender as it evidently was, would end with the sale.

At another auction which Vernon attended shortly after, the slaves sold presented a miserable appearance. They were nearly in a state of nudity and had evidently been half-starved. These had been kept in close confinement in the bilboes since they had been levied on, because they evinced a strong desire to return to the property from which they had been caught away by the Marshal entirely at random. But this was generally the case with those slaves sold for debt. They were levied on by the Marshal promiscuously when by any chance he could find the gate of the property open or, perhaps, when they went to market or were sent on errands. Frequently the boy and horse, or the wain, cattle and drivers were levied on, put up, and sold together. It was quite an ordinary thing for a gang of negroes cemented by every human tie and living together in their master's life time, to be sold for his debts immediately after his decease and thus become separated forever by a few strokes of the auctioneer's ruthless hammer.

Frequently, too, our young friend attended the 'Workhouse Sales'. Negroes taken up under the 'Vagrant Act' which prohibited persons of colour going abroad without a permit or their manumission paper. If one or the other of these documents was not produced the individual apprehended had an iron collar rivetted or locked around his neck and, by a stout iron chain five feet long, was fastened to another negro wearing the same badge of vagrancy; and this was invariably done on the strength of the negative proof which the non-production of their papers afforded. After having worked in chains for a given time they were probably sold unless, in the interim, they produced unequivocal proofs of their freedom or were claimed by their owners. When we bear in mind the little facility which their position offered (in chains at work by day, in the cell at night) of communicating with their friends – perhaps at a considerable distance; and further, that their friends belonged to the humble classes who would have little access to the public papers in which they were advertised, it requires no great stretch of the imagination to conceive that amongst the miserable convicts who sweated and toiled beneath the iron collar and the driver's whip, there were some who were as free by law, as a God of mercy and grace had made them by nature.

*V*ernon's health not mending, he visited the Milk River bath, a mineral spring on the south side of the island, celebrated for its medicinal virtues. A letter from a member of Assembly procured him lodgings at the buildings erected at the expense of the Island, near or over the spring; but he found that each visitor furnished his own board. As he travelled through the country his letters of introduction procured him several friends. Indeed everywhere he met with that courtesy and hospitality for which the West India Islands have ever been proverbial.

In the parish of St Ann's, justly esteemed 'the garden of Jamaica,' he spent several weeks with a family of the name of Hawkins. The head of the family had, several years before, given all his slaves their freedom. Most of them still remained labouring on his pen and received their wages weekly. From Mr Hawkins, Vernon gathered some particulars of the atrocities of slavery which he was quite unprepared to hear and which, from their nature, lie beyond the province and publicity. He stated that when he first settled in Saint Ann's, it was a very common thing for the slaves to be mutilated by sentence of the Slave Courts. Legs, arms, and ears were very frequently cut off as a punishment for running away; and this was not by law, or by the arbitrary conduct of a tyrannical master, but by judicial sentence.

'But,' observed Mr Hawkins, 'were you to state this in England on dixit it certainly would not be met with credit; we'll therefore take a ride to the Bay to-morrow. I am acquainted with the Clerk of the Peace, and in his office I'll show you the legal record.'

Next day the gentlemen visited the Bay and the Clerk of the Peace's office. After the usual compliments had passed, Mr Hawkins took a few turns about the room, occasionally stopping to look at some advertisements posted on the walls. At length he drew a book from the shelf and laying it down winked at Vernon and walked towards the legal functionary with whom he entered into conversation while his guest examined a part of the record. The book was handsomely bound in red Morocco, gold lettered with gilt edges. It was full of entries made in court and signed by the presiding magistrate and the clerk of the peace for the time being. The names of Stennett and Raffington figured on its pages. The following are a few of the sentences as they were recorded on its opening pages: –

'Dick, to Drax-Hall, for being an incorrigible runaway – guilty. Sentenced to have his right leg amputated beneath the knee. Valued at £30.

'Tom, to Seville, for running away – guilty. Sentenced to have his ears cut off, to receive nine and thirty lashes, and to be kept to hard labour in the work-house for six months, and to receive like number of lashes on being discharged.

'Cudjoe to New Ground for being an incorrigible runaway – guilty. Sentenced to be transported to Botany Bay. Valued at £15.

'Charles, an eboe, to Cardiff Hall, for running away – guilty. Sentenced to have his ears cut off and to be kept in close confinement until fit to work.

'William, a creole, to Mammee Bay, burglary and running away – guilty. Sentenced to have his right arm and one of his ears cut off. Valued £20.

The entire book was a record of these 'legalized barbarities'. Vernon threw it down in disgust as Mr Hawkins tapped him on the shoulder, intimating that it was time they should leave the office. As they journeyed home, Mr Hawkins related several barbarous murders that had been committed by masters on their slaves in the interior of the parish, but the perpetrators had in very instance escaped, slave evidence being inadmissible in the Colonial Courts of Law.

'There is [only] one solitary instance on record,' said Mr Hawkins, 'of a white man being executed for murder of a slave. The circumstance occurred in St James'. A white man moving in the higher walks of life was executed for shooting a slave called 'Mucco John'. But it was under extraordinary circumstances. The prosecution was instituted at the instance of the Deputy Marshal for the parish, by whom the negro was employed to scale Ledgendge's fence to facilitate a levy.

'The planter, Mr Vernon,' continued Mr Hawkins, as they sat over their wine in the evening; 'is just what the slave system makes him. Most of them come to this country early in life, when the mind may be easily moulded to any form. At this period their prejudices against slavery [are great].[20] But, as it was of old, even so is it now – "evil communication corrupts good manners". By association with scenes of horror, the feelings soon lose their keen edge, the moral sensitiveness is at last blunted, and the moral purity sullied; the mind lapses into a state of indifference from which the transit to actual guilt is easy, in a word, the heart becomes blunt. Self-interest ...[21] throws its influence into the scale. The planter now perceives that his philanthropy unfits him for the avocation he is destined to pursue; circumstances often prevent his return to his native land. He bows to the over-powering pressure of events and is hurried on with the stream. The only question asked, relative to the planter, by the attorney is, "Is he a good manager?" which means "Does he make large crops of sugar and rum?" In order to do this, the planter must goad on the slave: his only alternative is the driver's lash, but perhaps the question may be asked, "Will not the negro work without the whip?" I reply, neither the slave nor the free man will work without a stimulus to exertion. The testimony of every age and nation proves the assertion; the stimulant among free men is the love of wealth, honour and renown; the stimulant used with the slave is coercive measures – and the more powerful these are, the greater quantity of work is wrung out, the more brilliant are the manager's credentials and the higher he rises in his employer's esteem. I am convinced that there are many sugar estates that could not be carried on profitably, without the sacrifice of the lives of the slaves.'

'Then undoubtedly they should be abandoned,' said Mr Vernon.

'Yes, they will be abandoned,' said Mr Hawkins, 'if the bill now before the British Parliament becomes law, as God grant it may. [If it does not] these estates, which, to speak hyperbolically, have been manured with blood, like the ground cursed by the Almighty for the sin of Cain, will refuse to yield her strength.'

'The blush of shame reddens my cheek when I reflect that slavery is linked to the British Throne,' said Vernon; 'but my heart bleeds at every pore when I have in mind that it is linked also to my father's house. For generations past my ancestors have revelled in wealth that has been "the price of blood". I dreamt not of half the horrors of slavery until observation spread them before my eyes; and it is well it has been so, for I am now fully convinced that nothing but ocular demonstration would have convinced me that scenes so repugnant to the feelings of our common humanity were enacted in a country professedly Christian, and one forming an integral part of a nation standing in the foremost ranks of civilization, whose march in science, whose staunch Protestantism, has exalted her to such a status that she stands forth a model to the surrounding nations.'

'I am fully convinced,' replied Mr Hawkins, 'that were it possible to convey to the minds of the commonalty of England, a true picture of the barbarities that I have seen practised since my residence in Jamaica – the well authenticated tales of horror; of brutal seduction connected with the people of colour – they would rise up simultaneously and demand, I use the active verb, Mr Vernon, I say the people of England would demand that this foul stain on the escutcheon of their nation should be blotted out. If ever there was destruction that wasted at noonday, it is the system we are contemplating. Let its miserable advocates whitewash as they may, it's as black as the portals of hell. Let philosophers and moralists, with Dr Paley at their head, apply their soothing syrups and patent plasters as they can, the gangrene is visible in the whole social system; and even the slaveholder himself is not deceived by their wretched sophistry. Can He whose religion was a promulgation of "goodwill towards men", whose badge of discipleship is love, cease to frown upon a moral evil so fearful in its consequences, on a monster wearing on its shameless cheek the hue of blood, and in whose red right hand are the instruments of cruelty? The day may be distant, but it will come, when this demon will have no existence beyond the suburbs of Hell.'

Vernon's health having been restored, it was not without considerable reluctance that he parted with Mr Hawkins and his amiable family.

As Vernon felt an anxiety to see some parts of the interior of the country, he turned out of the carriage road on reaching the larger iron bridge that spans the Rio Cobre, and took a bridle track that led through the heart of the mountains into the parish of St George's; and ultimately, after meandering up mountainous defiles, along the edge of frightful precipices, down into the valleys and through innumerable streams that were tributaries to the Wag Water, the most dangerous river in the island, led to the little seaport town of Annotto Bay. In addition to the steep and rugged character of the road, it was in most places deep with mud, yet such was the beauty of the mountain scenery, the richness and variety of the flowers that grew spontaneously wherever the eye wandered, the melody of the feathered tribe as they poured forth their dulcet notes, the wild dash of water pouring from one scraggy eminence to another like sheets of molten silver, until at length reaching the deep glen below, it became united with the purling stream, on whose gentle surface was reflected the shadows of the huge rocks, or stately trees that reared themselves above. Such was the effect of this enchanting landscape on a mind like Vernon's peculiarly susceptible of physical beauty, that the shadows of evening gathered around and the chill of nightfall was felt, ere he began to reflect that it was time he thought of a resting place for the night. In the tropics there is little twilight; and the sun was hardly sunk in the west and the golden hue of its last ray been admired, when the sombre pall of night falls over the brilliant scene.

Vernon was now thoroughly aroused from his reverie by his servant Quinto who, riding as close up to him as the road would permit, enquired, 'Please Massa, where is you goin' please tap to-night?'

'Why, Quinto,' replied Vernon, 'I don't know exactly where we are to spend the night; perhaps we shall come to some place presently and I shall stop and request a lodging.'

'Yes, Massa, you mus' tap; de pass we da pon now no good,' said the boy.

'What do you mean?' enquired his master, 'by its not being good? Do you think that we are likely to be waylayed and robbed.'

'No dat altogeder, Massa, but place wa too much water da, no good ar night time,' replied Quinto.

'Are you afraid we shall be drowned?'

'No, Massa; drown would ar nutten, dat is a fare deat', and man can't fraid for deat'' when him time come,' replied the servant.

'Come now, Quinto, tell me the truth; what is it that you are afraid of?', quoth [sic] his master.

'Well, den, to tell Massar de gospel trute, dis yah is ar awful place fe duppy. No yerry dem da whistle all round we?', replied Quinto.

'What do you think they can do us?'

'If da catch we, da no we cary we in ar middle bush, 'trip we naked, tie we to tree, and feed we pon raw buds, elsin dead rat,' said Quinto. Vernon now laughed heartily.

'Hi, Massa, no laugh; duppy can't hear you laugh arter dem, an' me yerry de whistle da come closer; Massa can please ride fasser,' said the boy.

Vernon, knowing the boy would be left behind as he rode a lazy mule, started off as fast as he could go over such a road, and in a short time a turn in the road took him out of sight. As soon as he had lost sight of his master, Quinto set up such a yell that the very wood re-echoed with the sound. Vernon thereon halted and was laughing heartily when the frightened boy came up. He declared that the duppies had given him a frightful chase and, at length, seized hold of his mule's tail and, had not the mule sent up his heels and broken the duppy's jaw-bone he would certainly have fallen into their clutches. On his master's enquiry as to how he knew that the duppy's jaw bone had been broken, he replied:

'Hi, 'im no tap 'im whistle.'

'But how has that stop"t them all whistling?' enquired Vernon.

'De res' ar dem no mus' be tap whistle help men im jaw-bone,' replied the negro; 'we better try retch some place before dem begin whistle agen.'

The boy's yelling had alarmed some negroes who lived in the woods and one of them came out to see what was the matter and stood in the road with a lighted torch. On seeing this, Quinto made up [rode close up] to his master and, trembling dreadfully, began to mutter some kind of prayer. On Vernon's calling out and receiving a reply, the boy's fears vanished and he rode up to the man, from whom they learnt that there was a house a little before them, belonging to a pen, on which an overseer resided. Their informant, for a trifle, undertook to escort them thither and in a quarter of an hour they arrived at the place. Vernon was kindly received, but the house looked comfortless and promised little.

The property had been given up and was overgrown with bush, it carried a hundred head of cattle which the overseer said were 'attached' to the place; but as the fences had never been repaired for years past, the stock became very much 'detached' as the neighbouring planters knew, to their sorrow. The overseer was employed by an old lady who resided at a property in the neighbourhood; but so grinding were her terms that the planter was literally starving on his stipend. He had two children and their mother entirely dependent on him for support. The building was large and had evidently been once a splendid mansion and, from the remnants of elegance scattered throughout, must formerly have been handsomely kept and costly furnished.

It was late before anything in the shape òf supper made its appearance. At length, three or four pieces of dilapidated crockery were placed by the coloured woman who appeared to be servant of all work, on the table and Vernon was invited to partake of some refreshment by the overseer who excused himself on the score of a late dinner. On one plate there was a piece of roasted cod-fish, another contained a couple of herrings, while in the third there was some roasted plantains. The fish was as salt as brine and the vegetables had not yet arrived at perfection. Over so unsavoury a meal it is not to be supposed much time was spent. Yet, as Vernon felt convinced it was the best the house afforded he appeared to enjoy his repast and felt perfectly contented.

Early next morning, having partaken in a cup of warm milk and given the children each a piece of money, he took his departure. He continued his journey until nearly mid-day when dark clouds obscured the sun, the thunder rolled heavily overhead, and the lightning flashed fearfully around. It was evident that the dense clouds would shortly empty themselves in a torrent of rain, after which it would be impracticable to ford the swollen mountain torrents. This prospect induced Vernon to push his steed forward in order to reach a dwelling which appeared in a distance. At the door of this mansion he shortly arrived and a servant, having taken his horse into the stable, he ascended the stair-case which led into a large veranda. There he waited some time before the door was opened and a servant girl desired, in her mistress's name, that he would walk in. The house was sumptuously furnished. Several rooms through which Vernon passed before he reached the sanctum of the mistress were literally crammed with ottomans, couches, sofas, velvet fested [covered] chairs, pianos, harps, guitars, book-cases, centre-tables and easy chairs. The floors were either of highly polished woods, variegated, or covered with rich carpets; chandeliers hung from the centre of the ceiling, and the walls were tastefully hung with pier glasses and oil paintings. Some of the latter were of extraordinary size and no doubt of great value. The room occupied by the proprietress of this mansion, who was apparently near sixty, was small and furnished plainly; the windows were curtained with blue damask, richly figured, the ottomans covered with figured satin, the chairs with velvet and on each was embroidered the family crest in bright colours. The old lady sat before an elegant work-table elaborately carved, on which lay her work box and writing desk, richly inlaid with mother o' pearl. Vernon was received very kindly, and long before the tempest, which for a while raged fearfully, had ceased he felt himself quite at home with his entertainer, and cheerfully accepted an invitation to dinner. In the dining hall they were joined by the old lady's grand-daughter, her only companion. This young lady, who was introduced as Miss Secard, had apparently attained her eighteenth or twentieth year. She was of graceful mien, with features so exquisitely moulded that criticism itself must have pronounced her beautiful. Her eyes were rather languishing than bright and seemed to be a true index of her meek and quiet spirit. Her auburn hair fell in natural ringlets over her shoulders and appeared to set at defiance any attempts at improvements from art. Her conversation evinced that her mind had been highly cultivated, and her attainments in literature far from trifling.

In such company the time passed rapidly and it was past four in the evening ere Vernon spoke of his departure. Much to his surprise he was informed by the old lady that she had ordered a chamber to be prepared for him, as it was impossible for either man or beast to ford the river that ran between them and the next village. Under these circumstances Vernon felt very grateful for the accommodation offered. Time passed on very agreeably and all seemed surprised when the old clock in the entry struck ten. Indeed, Miss Secard said, she thought it was but nine and was only convinced to the contrary by ocular demonstration. The domestics then came into the hall, the young lady read a portion of Scripture, a short prayer followed, and the family retired for the night. Vernon, having closed his chamber door, threw himself into a chair and began to ruminate over the events of the day. Miss Secard had made an impression on his mind, and on her character he began to ponder. This young lady had shone in the drawing rooms of the aristocracy of London, revelled amidst the gaieties of Paris, travelled for years on the Continent, wandered amidst the ruins of the amphitheatre at Rome, and promenaded the deserted halls of the Alhambra, in Granada; yet here she was, buried amidst the snakes and bushes, without companions, without amusements, in the mountainous regions of an insignificant isle, and while thus she was cheerful, contented and happy and spent her time administering to the sick and poor. These musings might have continued much longer, and the impressions made on the mind of our young traveller become lasting, had it not so happened that the form and features of Celeste were ineradicably engraved upon the red leaved [sic] tablets of the heart. It was certain, however, that Miss Secard had his sincere esteem, and this was sufficient, for as a popular writer has observed. 'It is surprising what a close alliance there is between "love and murder", so would we also remark on the near affinity that exists between love and sincere esteem – provided always that this sincere esteem be entertained by a young man of five and twenty for a lovely girl of nineteen.

A comfortable night's rest and an early breakfast enabled Vernon to renew his journey with much pleasure next morning, though Quinto seemed much downcast from the assurance he felt that 'dar foot de wortless mule tek so kick duppy would neber car' em ketch home'. It carried him, nevertheless, that day as far as Port Maria, a picturesque village on the sea coast, where they remained for the night at a tavern that afforded excellent accommodation; and next day's journey brought them to Saint Ann's Bay. The horses and mule having strayed from the stable of the tavern during the night, Quinto went in search of them; and his master, finding that the lodging house library consisted of only one volume, which was 'The Ready Reckoner', strolled out to see the town and fell in with a sale of negroes. There were three brown girls, a stout sambo woman, a black boy and an old man. The girls were from twenty to twenty-five years of age, the woman past thirty, the boy about ten and the man grey headed. The girls seemed to be quite cheerful, the others looked dejected; all were very well dressed and in good health. As Vernon cast his eyes about the slave market, he noticed an elderly lady of very genteel appearance; but as she met his gaze, she seemed to shrink back with the usual delicacy of her sex. Presently she was accosted by a gentleman dressed as a trooper. A casual observer might have seen that this man prided himself not a little on his war-like habiliments, as holding his huge metal-cased sword under his arm he strutted at his ease. He was not the man, evidently, to waste much time in conversation with an old lady. In four minutes he stalked off as boldly as he had advanced; but a sentence that fell from his lips as he turned away attracted the attention of Vernon who, after a few overtures, began a little friendly chat with the old lady. Here never has yet been found an old lady that was deficient in the article of tongue. It is not, therefore, to be supposed that our present 'old lady' formed an exception to the general rule. Certainly no one who knew 'old Mrs Chitty' ever had any reason to think that she did. After informing Mr Vernon of the various wrongs, injuries, and acts of oppression she had undergone during her pilgrimage of many long years in this troubled and terrible world, she at length reached the climax of all her grievances, the one that had placed her in the position she that morning occupied among the bidders at the Marshal's sale. The sambo woman, she said, was her property: yes, she was sure she was, for she had bought and paid for her with her own hard cash, when she was only nine years of age, had brought her up as if she had been her own child. Then Mrs Chitty's feelings rose too big for endurance; she felt her grievances bubbling out of the corners of her small black eyes; and the 'old lady', as ladies, whether old or young, generally do in such cases applied her pocket handkerchief very sympathetically to her eyelids. She then proceeded. The girl lived with her until she had two children when her daughter, having changed her state of single blessedness, left the maternal roof to revel abroad in all the happiness that conjugal bliss and five hundred pounds could afford, taking by mutual consent the girl who was called Jessie to share her fortunes or, at least her misfortunes; for it was pretty clear that these had been neither few nor small since, as the 'old lady' said, her husband had 'taken to drinking', treated the wife very ill and squandered away her little fortune and, as it appeared, Jessie into the bargain, as she had been levied on for debt, with other goods and chattels which were that morning to be sold to the highest and best bidder. Now 'old Mrs Chitty' maintained that as Jessie had only been lent to her daughter, it was illegal to sell her for her debts, and as the old lady thought she was certainly the best bidder for Jessie, there she was in *propria persona* to do her best in the interest of all parties concerned. Vernon certainly thought that his new acquaintance was the best bidder, but as she had only fifty pounds tied up in the corner of the little hand kerchief, with which she had wiped her eyes occasionally, he entertained serious fears that she would not prove the highest. He, however, kindly promised to help the widow if her pounds fell a little short. Mrs Chitty then held a short confabulation with her friend the trooper, who requested several persons present not to bid against the 'old lady', as the woman belonged to her, and had been unjustly levied on for her daughter's debt.

The sale now commenced by several huge 'rummers' of mixed liquor being handed round to the most respectable of the party. The Marshal's Deputy – a bloated, ill-looking fellow, acted as crier.

The trooper bought the three girls for £200, a merchant of the Hebrew persuasion got the old man for £40, and the woman fell into the hands of her old mistress. There were no bidders for the poor boy as he had the yaws, a malignant disease very prevalent among negroes in the West India islands.

On Vernon's return, he received a very hearty welcome from the slaves and also from Jackson and Sparks. The former, he presented with a very handsome silver-mounted horsewhip, and the latter with a valuable percussion gun. Nor had he forgotten the servants that moved around him, for each he had procured a suitable present. Mary Ann came in for a pair of earrings, and a string of coral beads.

But it is now time that we should throw some light on the clandestine movements of Catherine Brown. These exegetical remarks will form part of our next chapter.

SIX

*T*he merchantmen that crowded the snug harbour of Falmouth were beginning to settle down in the water, laden with the sugar and rum which came pouring down from the various estates in the parish to the barquadier. As the last huge hogshead of sugar weighing little short of a ton, was hoisted on to the deck of the Clara, the sailors gave three hearty cheers that were heard distinctly by all on shore. The trusty old ships that had made so many transatlantic voyages laden with staples from the tropics, was now hauled out opposite the channel, her light sails were bent and sent aloft, the topsail sheet and halliard stretched along the deck; and did she not look noble, as she lay down to her bends in the water, with the blue-peter at her mast head, and the flag of 'old England' floating over her stern? This gallant bark was destined to bear Catherine and her child over the mighty ocean that rolled between her and the land of freedom.

'My dear Mrs Christie,' exclaimed Mrs Arnold as, gasping for breath, she threw herself into a chair; 'I am certainly at my wit's end; there has been Arnold hunting, until he has thrown himself into a fever, in search of a servant to purchase, and been disappointed at the last hour. That fool of a woman Foster has changed her mind and won't sell the girl we made ourselves sure of getting. Now it is impossible that we can sail with two children, without some female attendant.'

'My dear girl,' said the old lady, looking as cool as a cucumber, 'why can't you hire a slave and send her back?'

'Simply because Granville Sharp, long before my grandmother was born, decided that I should not.'

'True,' said the old lady, 'I had quite forgotten that.'

'What am I to do?' petulantly enquired Mrs Arnold.

'Trust in Providence,' calmly replied her amiable old friend.

'And the girl will drop through the sky?' said Mrs Arnold.

A servant entered and said that a person wished to speak to Mrs Christie.

'Do', said Mrs Arnold, 'say you are not at home'.

'That wouldn't be quite true, child,' replied the old lady. 'I will think for you as I go down, and be back in five minutes. Take some lemonade, it will refresh you,' and the old lady left the room.[22]

The individual who enquired for her was Catherine; and Mrs Christie, remembering Mrs Arnold's need, decided that she would just do. So after some arrangements Catherine and her baby were sent off with Mr and Mrs Arnold, for Catherine wanted to leave the island. At the last moment they all got on board, and the ship moved slowly out of the harbour. The shore seen from on board was beautiful. The town nestled in green, and further on the large bridge beneath which ran the beautiful Martha Brae which, after meandering through a large tract of country, here emptied its delightful water into the sea. The entire landscape was indeed worthy of the artist's pencil.

The wind now freshened up, a few heavy laden vessels came rolling in through the narrow channel, the heavy laden vessel mounted the billows, down she went again, groaned, and sped forward while every seaman stood motionless at his post.

'She's through the Triangles,' exclaimed the pilot, addressing the captain.

'You showed her nose nobly into that last swell,' returned the captain.

'The sea breeze is on us,' said the pilot.

'Earlier than usual,' answered the Captain.

'Stand by your foretack and low-line,' roared the pilot.

'Aye! Aye! Sir,' answered the mate.

'Hard a-lee,' thundered the pilot.

'Hard a-lee,' responded the mate.

Gallantly the vessel answered her helm and tacked for a moment in the wind's eye, the mainsail, and every stitch of canvas filled with the fresh seabreeze that was prowing down, the water foamed around her bow, the jolly tars gave three cheers, and in ten minutes the pilot's boat was seen falling rapidly in the rear.

Leaving Catherine for the present to pursue her voyage to the land of freedom, we return to the affairs of the estate.

Jackson now appeared to be an altered man in many respects. At times he was moody, shy and dry, cold and selfish, and then, throwing off his melancholy he would be quite jovial and join eagerly with his former associates in pitching quoits, playing tricks or drinking.

'There's Dickens coming up the hill, by George!' exclaimed Fidler as he sat in the little portion at the head of the stairs smoking a cigar, in company with Jackson. 'What shall we do to get some fun out of the chap?'

'Get him drunk,' said Jackson.

'That won't do,' returned Fidler, handing his silver snuff-box to his companion as he spoke, 'we can't do much with one drunke[n] fellow, besides Dickens never gets drunk alone.' 'Give him twelve grains of tartar emetic.' said Jackson.

'The very thing,' answered Fidler.

All the rum was thrown *form* the decanter except about a drink. In this was shaken up twelve grains of tartar emetic.

'D -d hot,' said Dickens as he entered mopping the perspiration *form* his face; 'get us some cool water, Jackson, and let's have some grog.'

'I dare say you can drain a drink out of that old decanter until we get some more,' said Jackson, reaching for the water.

'Thank you,' answered Dickens, emptying the dose of emetic into his glass. He then filled his tumbler with water and swallowed its contents.

'Anything stirring? How many hogsheads last week?' enquired Dickens.

'Dull as death,' answered Jackson; 'seven hogsheads up to yesterday.'

'How's Sparks getting on in the still-house? Hope he's keeping himself up,' said Dickens.

'That's hard for poor Glass-Eye with the liquor staring him in the face eternally,' chimed in Fidler, handing the silver snuff box to Dickens.

'Can't stop,' said Dickins. 'Want to get over to Jaw-Bone-Jacks to dinner. Here, Tom, run for my horse (making a cut at Sambo with his supplejack).

Dickens rode off, and Jackson and Fidler watched him with a grin. At the top of the hill they saw him stoop forward, and presently he stooped forward again, and then turned his horse's head back.

'By George,' said Fidler 'it's acting,' and the planters laughed with all their might. Dickens reached the house and alighted, exclaiming: 'I am a 'What's the matter?' said Jackson, endeavouring to suppress the visible dead man; I am a dead man.' muscles of his face.

'What the devil's the matter?' exclaimed Fidler wiping the tears that trickled down his cheeks.

'It's all over,' said Dickens, bringing off a huge mouthful, and then half a dozen more.

'Hell fire!' exclaimed Fidler, 'the man is poisoned.'

'Don't swear!' ejaculated Dickens. 'I am dying; its all over, send for the Doctor, and get... [?]. O Lord, have mercy on me.'

Another deluge followed and then the sick man was got to bed.

'I've been a great sinner,' continued Dickens. 'O Lord! O Lord! Jackson, you must make my will.'

'Drink this,' said Jackson handing him some lukewarm water; 'and keep a bold heart. A man can die but once, you know.'

Dickens swallowed the water and vomited in good earnest.

'Look up, old boy,' said Fidler, who had been nearly choked with laughing in the entry. 'Perhaps you'll be on your pins again, the Doctor will be here directly.'

'It's all over; it's all over,' said the sick man despondently. 'Hand the basin, hand the basin.'

By this time Doctor Dick had ridden up from Salt Marsh, a small hamlet two miles below the estate, and entered the house with an air of consequence.

'Your servant, Mr Jackson,' said Doctor Dick.

'Your most obedient,' replied the overseer.

'Hope you are well, Doctor,' said Fidler handing him the silver snuffbox.

This worthy son of Aesculapian was then duly informed of the disease under which his patient laboured. He laughed heartily, promised to back them in the joke, swallowed a tumbler of strong grog and attended to Dickens.

'Hello Dickens!' said the Doctor, 'what's the matter?'

'Poisoned!' said Dickens with a heavy groan.

Doctor Dick placed his finger on his pulse and looked occasionally at his large old-fashioned watch, winking at Jackson with the corner of his eye. He then weighed him out a pretty large dose of calomel and jalop and, returning to the hall, sat down to dinner. By the time the worthy party had emptied their dozen glasses each, poor Dickens was sadly disturbed. About midnight he took some gruel and fell asleep, and the day after returned to his estate.[23]

The crop continued with its usual every-day routine of common-place events. The panting oxen moved slowly into the mill-yard with the heavy laden wagons, the tired mules trotted round in the mill, the cane and trash carriers passed and re-passed each other, the boiler-men brushed the scum off the boiling cauldrons with their broad skimmers and ladled about the hot syrup with their deep bright copper ladles, the stoker-man shoved up his huge fire, the drivers cracked their whips, the boys sung [sic], and the overseers talked just as loud and as fast as they had done months before. Nothing disturbed the dull monotony, or gave respite to the systematic drudging existing on Greenside Estate. At length, crop was over and the huge hogsheads of sugar and puncheons of rum rack, branded G.C. with Gattop, were safely lodged at Barquadier.

The Friday after was appointed for the 'crop over ball' and great preparations were made in the way of solids and liquids for the occasion. The overseer's hall was ornamented tastefully with bunches of flowers and lit brilliantly by wooden candlesticks hung against the wall. The neighbouring overseers met at a grand dinner party and several of their mistresses made their appearance about dusk. The girls and young men in holiday costume assembled as soon as the room was lit. Among the gentlemen 'Mass George' figured and Mary Ann took undisturbed rank with the Busha's ladies and, much to their chagrin, led off the dance with the gallant Mr Fidler, she being a kind of legal representative *pro tem* of Catherine Brown who was absent without leave. About one o'clock, the gentlemen were seen fast asleep in various places and positions, having paid very ardent devotions at the Shrine of Bacchus. Our friend Sparks, alias 'Glass-Eye', at a much earlier hour of the evening, measured his length beneath the entry table and remained in quiet possession until disturbed by the house girl whose duty it was to spread the table for breakfast next morning. The light coloured girls now left and the field negroes, who are considered of lower caste than the domestics, and who had been dancing reels and cutting all kinds of capers in the entry and around the house wherever the sound of the fiddle could be heard, now took their turns in the hall and, superintended by Vernon, kept it up until sunrise.

A short time after crop, Mr Fleming visited the estate. As usual, Vernon was asked to dinner at the Great House. Tempted by the beauty of the evening, the attorney with his young friend strolled into the garden. Almost mechanically the old gentleman's footsteps glided along a little track in the grass which led directly to the grave on which rested the marble slab. Here they stopped and there was a total pause in conversation which is not uncommon while the eye rests, as it were, on the mouldering ashes of the dead. At length, the silence was broken by Mr Fleming, who said with a tone of deep feeling: 'This, Mr Vernon, is the grave of my wife.'

'I thought ... I thought ... I was told,' said Vernon in a tone of surprise, 'that it was the grave of Celeste's mother.'

'So it is, Mr Vernon,' replied the old gentleman, much excited, 'Celeste is my daughter.'

Vernon was speechless with surprise.

'I see,' continued Mr Fleming, 'that what I have communicated has produced astonishment and I do not wonder at it as no soul on earth, except the old clergyman by whom we were united, is in possession of the secret I have just communicated to you. There were two others privy to the transaction but they are now, where, in the course of nature, I shall ere long myself be – in the grave. I am anxious, however, before I am borne to the latter, to communicate particulars to you, who stand prominently forward among the few to whom I would commit a secret, that I particularly wish should be kept from the knowledge of my family, at least during the lifetime of my present wife. With your permission, I will relate to-morrow full particulars and commit to your care one or two documents, and I desire that on your return to England you will produce them to your father who is one of my earliest friends and corroborate the testimony which they bear by the declaration which I have this evening made.

Vernon, having thanked the old gentleman for the honour he had conferred by committing to his trust a secret of such moment, pressed his hand warmly and they returned to the house.

'Who would look at the grave, cool, calculating, old Mr Fleming, and for a moment imagine that there was any romance connected with him?' thought Vernon when he found himself alone that evening and began to ruminate on what had transpired in the garden. That Celeste was a girl of colour, he felt convinced, and from his personal knowledge of the deep prejudices entertained by Mrs Fleming on the complexional question, he saw at once the barrier that prevented her being introduced into the attorney's family. However, he felt happy that so far as the veil of obscurity had been raised and facts developed, they tended directly to move many fears he had entertained for the ultimate welfare of Celeste and it was the deepest interest that he listened on the following evening to the old gentleman's story.

Chapter

SEVEN[24]

'The mother of Celeste,' said the Attorney, 'was the daughter of a proprietor in the parish of St James. She, with her sister had been educated under the care of their aunt in England. She was seventeen and her sister twenty when they returned to the island. Their father had intended that they should again have visited his native land but circumstances over which the old gentleman could exercise no control altered very materially his primitive arrangements concerning his daughters. With their father, they resided entirely in the shade, the prejudices of colour imperatively excluding them from the circle in which, at least by education, they were qualified to move. I was their father's attorney and overseer at the time these girls returned to their paternal home and, as such, had an opportunity of an intimate acquaintanceship. Sophia the [older], was beautiful and fair as the lily; there was not the slightest appearance in her complexion of the dark blood that coursed through her veins. Charlotte, though fair, looked dark beside her sister, but her more amiable disposition made ample amends for any deficiency that existed in her external appearance. As she was in person the very prototype of her daughter, so she possessed entirely her meek and quiet spirit.'

Here the old gentleman manifested some feeling and opened a small casket from which he took a miniature painting of a female whose [similarity] to Celeste convinced Vernon of the truthfulness of the artist's pencil. There were the sweet light blue eyes; the dark brown hair and the meek expression of the living picture.

'I soon formed an attachment to Charlotte,' resumed the Attorney, 'which I at length endeavoured to throw off as circumstances which I had not at first weighed pressed themselves on my mind. To have offered her less than marriage would, I felt fully assured, have secured nothing but her

90

scorn and contempt. To have formed a matrimonial alliance with one born of a slave, would bring down on my head the curse of a father whom I had ever reverenced and obeyed. For nearly two years I struggled on, at one time using all my endeavours to win her affections and at other times absenting myself from her company for weeks. At length, my honoured father died in his 60th year, leaving me a slender feature.[25] This barrier having been removed, I shortly after made proposals which were accepted by Charlotte and approved by her father. These terms were a settlement and a private marriage. Every arrangement had been made and the day had been decided on for our union; but in the order of Divine Providence, her father was called suddenly away. Much to the astonishment of every one acquainted with the old gentleman's business habits, he died intestate – at least no will was ever found. Shrewd suspicions, however, were thrown out that the will had been suppressed by an interested party, but this was a matter of speculative opinion. As Charlotte and her sister were illegitimate children, the whole of their father's property fell to his nephew, a young man of libertine principles and practice who had gained for himself an unenviable notoriety by seducing one of his near relatives.[26]

'Into the hands of this wretch,' said Mr Fleming with emotion, 'the property that really belonged to these girls fell. I determined, however, by marriage, to place myself in a position to become their protector as they now stood isolated in the world and, accordingly, made arrangements for my union. The legal gentleman, however, whom I had employed to transact the marriage settlement to procure the special license, etc., aroused me one morning at two o'clock, having ridden all night, and informed me of a circumstance that filled me with consternation. He had discovered that Charlotte and Sophia were slaves. They never had been legally manumitted and were as much the property of the nephew as the cattle that turned the mill. The two accomplished Miss Hawthorns were, after all, only, in the eye of the law, mere things, goods and chattels, which, with the oxen and mules, were to be delivered up to the heir-at-law. For half an hour after the reception of this intelligence, I remained as a man in a trance. The lawyer spoke, I saw his lips moving, but not a sound was heard. At length, I heard my named called but found it impossible to articulate. There was a buzzing in my ears and I saw objects dimly. Mr Myers shook me violently by the shoulder, aroused me to consciousness and I looked on the real scene.

'This, Sir,' said my informant, 'is the time for action; what can be done?'

'We must do something, Mr Myers,' I replied, 'to save the girls. Sooner would I blow out their brains than hand them over to that brutal heartless wretch who has written to forbid that they should touch an article of their father's plate.'

'So would I,' replied the lawyer. 'But a thought has struck me. Listen: the tax account against the property has not been paid. Persuade the Collecting Constable to levy on the young ladies, put them up for sale and, do, you buy them in.'

'Good Heavens!' I replied, 'put up Charlotte and Sophia at public auction!'

'It is the only chance,' replied Mr Myers, 'of saving them from worse. Jack Hawthorn landed in town yesterday, I was informed by the post this morning. If these girls fall into his hands they will be ruined or die in the dungeon; we cannot interfere between the master and his slave. I say, then, see the collecting constable; he is your relative and an honest man. Let him make his levy to-day and sell to-morrow.'

'I could suggest no better plan. By mid-day the levy had been made and, on the day following, the girls were sold at public out-cry and bought in by Myers for me; and full well do I recollect that, as we drove home that evening, I cursed slavery in my heart. The next day our marriage took place. Under all the circumstances of the case you will not be surprised that it was strictly private as I had many relatives whose feelings I was anxious to spare. For several years we resided in St James. Our conjugal bliss was uninterrupted. On my appointment to the Cunningham estates as Attorney, my wife was sent to this place and business of importance carried me at the same time to Kingston where, as witness in a Crown case, I was detained a fortnight. During this separation she died in giving birth to Celeste. Her sister, for whom I provided, went to England and for a while resided with her aunt. She, at length, married. Since then I have lost sight of her as she went to travel on the Continent. Her aunt died a short time prior to this event. It is my earnest desire that you should, if possible, on your return home, discover if she is alive, as I am anxious Celeste should be placed under her protection. Sophia's husband's name I never learnt.'

The Attorney, having concluded his story, committed to Vernon's care several memorandums and documents together with Charlotte's miniature which, he knew, would be useful in prosecution of the discovery he desired to be made and, which, for reasons fully understood by the reader, he had no desire should fall into the hands of the family by his second marriage.

About this time, great excitement was caused on the estate in consequence of the brutal treatment of an old man belonging to the property, by a neighbouring overseer. 'Father Williams', as he was called by the slaves, was regarded by all who knew him as far above the ordinary character of the negro. Had Williams worn a white skin he would have been the very beau ideal of a 'nice old man'. As he happened, however, to be identified with 'the servile progeny of Ham', he was, as a matter of course, 'little and unknown'. Williams had been, in that quarter, a kind of 'first fruit' of missionary enterprise. This conversion to Christianity, and consequently consistent walk in life, had commanded respect from the white persons who knew him, while his attainments in Biblical knowledge raised him high in the estimation of his fellow slaves. But Williams, by some at least, will be regarded as 'worthy of double honour' when they learn the indefatigable labour, the untiring zeal with which he prosecuted his study of the volume that was destined to make him wise unto salvation. He was past fifty before the 'Sun of Righteous arose' upon him 'with healing in its wings', before he 'heard the joyful sound' – for 'how could he hear without a preacher?' True, there were a few clergymen of the Episcopal Church in the island but the negro formed no part of his charge. Sunday was the great day of business. The wholesale merchant, the grocer and spirit-dealer alike, threw wide open their doors and spread forth their merchandise. The slaves, by thousands, rushed to the market towns with vegetables, eggs, fruit, sugar and coffee which they had either raised in their gardens or stolen from their masters. Overseers, bookkeepers, and hundreds of housekeepers took advantage of this 'main chance' to supply themselves with necessaries or luxuries for the week; and when, in the evening, the stores had been closed and the market place evacuated, the military band played lively airs of 'the highest circle', promenaded the green while a troop of drunken seamen and soldiers kept the towns in an uproar till a late hour at night. Under such a state of things, and when it is borne in mind that the instructions of the slaves on the plantations were strictly prohibited by the heavy penalties of the law, can it be a matter of surprise that 'darkness covered the land, and gross darkness the people'?

But I return from my digression. Williams had, by performing several acts of kindness for the bookkeepers on the estate, prevailed on them occasionally to give him a few hints to his 'better understanding of the alphabet' and, in a short time, was enabled to prosecute his studies in private. His duties as head carpenter kept him constantly employed during the day, and he was unable to follow the example of some students of renown who 'burnt the midnight oil' for this very substantial reason that oil among the slaves was an [unobtainable article]. But the old man was too intent on his object to be foiled by difficulties, though almost [insupportable]; and notwithstanding it was impossible for him to procure oil to feed the lucid flame, he thought it practicable to scale the mountains in search of torch, a kind of wood peculiar to West India islands which burns with a brilliant light. Having procured an ample supply of this material, he sunk [sic] a common bottle half way in the ground in the centre of his hut. He could not have placed it on a stand without bringing the flaming torch too nearby in contact with the thatched roof. Under this light, the old man lay with his New Testament, often till midnight. The ultimate result of this diligence and perseverance was that 'Father Williams' could, at the end of the year, read many chapters without much spelling; and, indeed, it was said and, what was better still, fully believed by the large majority of his 'massa's negroes', that 'Farder Williams could 'splain and tell de wud mosin as well as de minister himself.' Poor Williams! Many a hard flogging and dismal confinement he underwent for exercising his clerical attainments. He was accused constantly of keeping the negroes up when they should have been asleep and putting 'nonsense into their heads' It was quite true that Father Williams' exhortations, like many in his line more eminent in their attainments were rather long-winded but then, as he said, 'the people had better be listening to him than carousing and dancing'.

At length, the drivers sided entirely with Williams, the overseers became tired of punishing the old man and the new attorney forbade his being interfered with. Williams' persecutions gained for him a degree of popularity and he was invited by the slaves on the neighbouring estates to extend his ministrations to them; and after he had finished his labours at dark, he would visit properties four or five miles distant and, at length, he was the means of persuading some hundreds of the slaves to give up their marketing on Sunday and visit chapel to hear the word of God; and it is only charity to hope that some of these believed, to the saving of their souls. At length, as I already stated, Father Williams gained a kind of notoriety even with the white people on the estates, where he was known, who treated him with a degree of attention and even respect.

On the occasion in question, the old man visited the slaves on an adjoining property, the overseer of which had determined to offer the most strenuous opposition to any inroads on his conservative principles. He was often heard to declare that 'he never would forsake the religion of his forefather,' but, as his neighbours were in total ignorance of his genealogy, so of course his religious creed was quite an enigma. It was pretty clear, however, that although he had emigrated from the northern part of Britain, his 'forefathers' had never mustered in the ranks of the old 'Cameronians'. Indeed, there were some so uncharitable as to insinuate

94

very scandalous suspicions as to his 'forefathers'. But with these innuendoes, the chronicler could not interfere, lest his impartiality should be impugned. This man, having learnt that Father Williams was at the negro houses singing and praying in direct opposition to his mandate on the subject, caused him to be apprehended and placed in the stocks for the night and, at 'shell-blow' next day, the usual hour of flogging, the old man was brought forward.

> His head was white and his eyes were dim.
> And his face was marked with woe
> The vigour of youth had passed by him,
> And labour had bent him low.

But neither his miserable nor emaciated appearance excited the sympathy of the brute in human form. Williams was severely flogged and, because he would not promise to refrain from visiting the estate in future, the man who 'forsook not the religion of his forefathers' jumped upon his body as it lay extended on the ground and blasphemously swore that he would trample the Holy Ghost out of him. The old man ultimately died from the effects of this brutality and when the matter was brought forward, one of the Judges of the land, who disgraced the ermine, stifled enquiry.

Chapter

EIGHT

*T*he death of Williams, as had been foreseen, produced no trifling
sensation on Greenside. The slaves manifested their grief in the
most frantic manner and their anger by acts of the most flagrant
insubordination. The large majority refused to obey the sound of the shell
which called them at the usual hour to labour. Those deemed the ringleaders
were brought at once under the ordeal of the lash, but it soon became
manifest that this was a case in which the stimulus of concise measures
was more than likely to prove abortive and the overseer seemed unwilling
to add the last drop to the waters of bitterness which seemed just ready to
overflow. More than a hundred slaves surrounded the overseer's dwelling,
manifesting every symptom of boisterous grief and calling for satisfaction.
At a late hour, they retired to their cottages, but early next morning returned
to the post they had occupied on the previous day and, in sullen silence,
awaited the arrival of the Attorney to whom Jackson had despatched a
message with tidings of the insurrectionary movements that were
developing.

A little after noon, Mr Fleming arrived at the scene of action … [and]
… the negroes renewed their barbarous manifestations. Some time elapsed
before he could gain for himself a hearing. At length, something like order
having been restored, he began to soothe their irritated passions and, at
length, succeeded in throwing oil upon the troubled waters. He promised
that the matter should undergo legal investigation and that a tomb should
be erected for the old man; that an allowance of sugar and rum should be
served out; and that a great 'wake' held that night should be followed by a
holiday, after which they should return to their several avocations.

The 'wake' and funeral passed off highly to the satisfaction of everyone
whom it concerned; and the fullest reliance being placed in the Attorney's
promise of prosecuting the matter and erecting a tomb, things immediately

returned to their accustomed level. As, however, Williams had met with his death unfairly, they could not believe that his spirit was at rest but that it 'wandered from its place'. They therefore, determined, as usual in such cases, to 'dance Myal and catch the shadow'.

The first step is in this important affair was to procure the direction and advice of the 'Obeah Man'. This recluse was the very dread of his fellow slaves, from the firm conviction that he held communion with the spirits of the departed and that he possessed the power of producing death by inflicting on his victims the most loathsome and lingering diseases. He resided on an estate called Orange Valley, about six miles distant from Greenside, was an African, and had, from his advanced age, become exempt from labour. In a dark forbidding-looking glade on the extreme confines of the property, this individual had erected his isolated hut; he lived entirely alone; no one was even permitted to enter his domicile nor, indeed, were any ever desirous of doing so unless they required the aid of his occult art. In such case, the visit must be made by a maiden and at the hour of midnight.

For several evenings the slaves assembled at the house where Williams had died for the purpose of appointing a delegate, but no maiden of character and courage volunteered. On their fourth meeting Rosallie, a remarkably handsome black girl, came forward boldly from the crowd and declared herself willing to undertake the unenviable mission. Her daring resolve was lauded by all present. That a girl of her shy and retired habits should, without compulsion, undertake such a task, was deemed very remarkable. The old women vowed she would live to receive rich presents from her grand-children; the old men united in wishing they had such a daughter, while the young men gathered around her and kissed her hands. But none among the crowd looked on with a prouder mien than Quinto, the favoured lover of the pretty Rosallie.

As soon as darkness brooded over the plains the next evening, Rosallie, with her accepted lover and a few chosen companions, directed their steps towards the property on which the 'obeah man' was located. As it was some time before midnight when they reached the estate, they remained with some of the people of Orange Valley until the proper hour arrived for visiting the recluse. The purpose that had brought them there occasioned no surprise; they admired the daring spirit of Rosallie and bestowed on her their united benedictions. Quinto and several others accompanied the young negress until they came in full sight of the hut. Here they halted and Rosallie with undaunted step proceeded alone. Just as the loud crowing of the cock announced that the hour had arrived, when 'Graves do yawn and churchyards give up their dead'. The intrepid girl knocked for admission at the door.

'You too late,' replied the obeah man; 'cock crow done.'

'No, Farder,' returned Rosallie, 'cock jus' crow.'

'Go pickney,' returned the African, 'an tan pon de white 'tone by de gate; if cock crow agen you can come.'

Rosallie took her stand on the huge rock near the wicket and directly chanticleer, for the second time, poured forth his clarion note. She returned; the old man opened his small door and she was admitted.

As the door closed and Rosallie felt herself all alone in an isolated position with an individual of whom, from childhood, she had heard so many wonderful accounts, terror took possession of her mind, her courage began to fail, an involuntary shudder came over her as she thought she had placed herself in the power of such a man. What if he should take advantage of her unprotected position! True, Quinto was within hearing; but how did she know how far the 'obeah man's' power extended? Perhaps he could, by his secret charms, prevent her raising any alarm; or he might be able by a word or a look, to paralize the efforts put forth by her lover or her companions in her behalf. This would be a trifling exercise of his power in comparison with the wonders she had heard related of him. She felt she stood on 'ticklish' ground, the cold sweat gathered on her brow, her feet tottered beneath her weight, and her frame quivered with agitation.

While these feelings passed rapidly through the maiden's mind, the old African had lit a lamp from a fire that blazed in the centre of his hut, placed it on a table and, seating himself on the only stool the place afforded, beckoned Rosallie to a seat on a kind of a bed which more nearly resembled the lair of some beast than the couch of a human creature. The African's first enquiry was 'if she had touched salt for that day?' He declared that if she deceived him in this matter, the consequences would be dreadful to her. Rosallie, having satisfied the enquiries in this and some other matters, was permitted to enter upon the business that had brought her to his hut and paid his fee of eight dollars: whereon the dealer in 'obeah' agreed to visit Greenside on the night appointed and the young negress took her departure. She was soon joined by Quinto and her companions who were happy to find that no injury had resulted from her adventure with one whom they believed to be possessed of supernatural powers.

On a bright star-light night, shortly after Rosallie's visit, an elderly negro was seen walking slowly through an unfrequented track that led from the high way to the negro cottages of Greenside Estate. A coarse woollen overcoat reaching from his neck to his ankles and closely buttoned rendered every other part of his dress invisible. He wore sandals and an old felt hat. At his right side hung a basket (called by the negroes a bankra) and, on the left, a short knife in a leather belt. He was supported, as he moved forward, by a long staff. This was 'Magungee' the obeah man of Orange Valley.

At a considerable distance from the suburbs of the plantation a large spot of ground had been cleared of the stunted brushwood and the inequalities so far levelled as to admit of dancing. The trees that grew here were of extraordinary dimensions and, blending their branches together, rendered the spot a delightful retreat from the burning rays of the noonday sun. Indeed, so closely had the twigs become entwined in their luxuriant growth with one another that neither the moon nor star light could penetrate the deep foliage. But it was neither the romantic appearance of this spot nor its isolated position that rendered it the favourite retreat of the slaves when superstition prompted them to revel in the lascivious[27] dancing or indulge in their nocturnal orgies. Their predilection for the spot arose entirely from the circumstance of their belief that the large cotton tree that reared its majestic head so far above every other that it 'wore the honours of the grove alone', was possessed of life, that it frequently performed long journeys at night. Though these peregrinations were performed in the most clandestine manner, yet some of the slaves that had been born with a call and who were, therefore, much more familiar with things supernatural than others possibly could be, had met the cotton tree as it moved with measured tread (like Pompey in his latter day 'supported by his weight alone'), busy as they believed, in the most momentous affairs connected with themselves. This cotton tree they regarded as a bona fide friend, knelt around it and uttered their complaints, bound themselves by solemn engagements beneath its shade and poured forth costly oblations at its root.

Preceded by the Obeah Man about fifty adults of both sexes proceeded at dead of night to this locality, several lamps having been suspended to the branches of the trees. Magungee began to play very slowly on the 'gumba' (a fantastic little drum), and the Myal dance commenced. The dancers were all but in a state of nudity. The obeah man had placed on a stool in the centre of the ring a coffin about a foot in length, in which was to be placed the shadow, when 'caught'. Around this they danced. They [then] threw themselves into the most ridiculous postures imaginable. It was impossible for the eye to follow their subtle and frantic movements. At one moment they remained nearly still, only tramping with their feet; the next they shot forward with a velocity truly surprising. Now they threw themselves down and lay sprawling on the ground and then, leaping up, sprang wildly into the air, the wily African assuring them over and over that the shadow was in the midst of them and insisting on them to 'ketch it'. However, in spite of their exertions and his exertions and exhortations, the shadow was not 'caught' that night. As soon as the morning star appeared in the east, the Myal dance ceased, and the Obeah Man, having scattered rat's bones, dog's teeth, the skin of the yellow snake chopped in atoms, human hair, eggshells, and poured out a bottle of sea-water, took his departure, assuring the slaves that the articles thus scattered would keep the 'shadow' from leaving the spot until they could dance again.

Neither the conjurer nor his deluded associates appeared to suffer any chagrin from the ill-success that had attended their previous nocturnal engagement. That the shadow of Williams was 'wandering' there could now be no longer any doubt; it had been decoyed to the cotton-tree by the Myal drum and, though it had eluded their grasp, yet it had been distinctly seen. Indeed, it was wonderful to hear how very adroitly it had escaped many who made themselves sure of having had a grim hold of it. Some had danced with it for several minutes together but, on making a grasp [at it], were surprised to find their hands full of one of their neighbour's hair. Others threw themselves on it; but on reaching the ground, the shadow was gone, and there was nothing between them and the cold ground save some stone or stump; the sweat streamed down their naked limbs, and they hooted and screamed. The obeah man said that the 'shadow' was a 'knowing one'; it was 'no boy'; it had slipped through his fingers twice.

As it was absolutely necessary for the happiness of the departed, as well as the peace of the entire slave population of Greenside that the shadow should be 'caught', it was determined that the Myal dance should be renewed on the following Saturday night and it was proposed to furnish the men with rum in order that they might dance with greater zest. The women were not so well pleased when Magungee directed that they were to drink a [concoction] of the 'Myal bush', as it was bitter and nauseous in the extreme, but from this decision there was no appeal.

The full moon had risen far up in the western sky and poured forth brilliantly its silver beams before the Myal dance commenced on the appointed evening. The old African [the Obeah Man], having killed a white fowl, sprinkled the blood over the ground on which they were to dance. He also strewed about some of the dust brought from Williams' grave. These preliminary arrangements were followed up by drinking – the men rum, the women 'Myal bush' tea. This was drunk from calabash cups, no other being allowed in use on any of these occasions; and each individual had to make a solemn oath before the Obeah Man that his or her cup had never been used for any other purpose whatever, nor ever been brought in contact with salt. The females had finished their 'bitter tea' some time before the men had dispatched their quantum of grog; and Magungee took his seat over the Myal drum. Dancing commenced in good earnest by the men whose movements seemed much increased by the rum; the women looked sulky, and it was evident their tea had not produced an exhilarating effect.

After some hours spent in dancing, leaping and gesticulating, the Obeah Man entered the ring, opened his little coffin and, giving a spring, succeeded much to the satisfaction of everyone, 'in catching the shadow'. The lid was then tied down with some pieces of black string, the coffin taken to the grace of old Williams and buried in the presence of all the slaves on the property. As this last rite of degradation and heathenish superstition was concluded, the light dawned on the morning of the Lord's Day.[28]

A few weeks after this affair of old Williams, 'Glass Eye' was promoted to the dignified position of overseer and, as was customary on such occasions, a kind of farewell dinner was given a day or two previous to his leaving Greenside for his new field of action; and several neighbouring overseers, who had known Sparks as overseer before, were invited to grace the festivities. Drinking, as usual, was the order of the day. Now Granger and Sparks had been for years rivals in the art of distillation and frequently had sparrings on the subject. When sober, they argued and laughed as they contended for victory; but being now under the excitement of liquor, fermentation was added to distillation, and clamour and declamation usurped the legitimate rights of logic and argument. 'What percentage of molasses do you give your cisterns in crop time?' asked Granger doggedly.

'Ten to be sure,' replied Sparks.

'How much dunder?' further enquired Granger, with the same morose air.

'A good deal of dunder,' replied Sparks.

'That's the reason that Greenside rum stinks so horribly; you can swear to it by the smell. I tell you what, 'Glass Eye', you know a d-d sight more about drinking rum than you do about making it,' said Granger.

'If you hadn't drunk new rum from the still, your rascally nose that looks like a piece of Burbon cane-top would not be now so full of grog blossoms,' returned Sparks.

'What are a few pimples on a fellow's nose compared to a pair of eyes that were borrowed from a wild cat,' said Granger, looking very savage.

'They are right down grog-blossoms,' returned Sparks, 'I can smell Maxfield rum oozing out of them.'

'You are a d-d liar, that's what you are, and no mistake, Mr Stokehold!' exclaimed Granger in a violent passion.

Sparks, following the advice of Chesterfield, sprang over the table to knock down his antagonist. The rest of the party who had been enjoying the fun, now interrupted.

'You wouldn't think of fighting with fists, gentlemen,' said Fidler.

'Of course not,' replied Jackson. 'My pistols are always at the service of any gentlemen that wish to use them.'

'To be sure,' said Sparks. 'Do you think I am going to fight with fists like a rascally negro? Doctor, will you be my second?'

'Poz!' replied Dr Dick, bringing down his fist on the table.

'And I'll back you up; d-n my eyes if I don't!' exclaimed Dickens.

'You'll see fair-play, Doctor,' said Sparks.

'Poz!' reiterated the man of physic, throwing back his chair and rising from the table.

'I'll shoot him as dead as a herring,' said Sparks, staggering and buttoning up his coat.

'I always suspected you never had any brains, but we'll see when I blow your ugly calabash to pieces presently,' returned Granger hiccoughing badly.

Meanwhile, Jackson and Fidler had loaded the pistols with powder and wad and, coming into the hall, laid them on the table.

'I move, gentlemen,' said Jackson, 'for a drink before fighting.'

'And a pinch of snuff,' said Fidler, handing forth his silver box.

'Poz!' said the Doctor. 'I second the motion.'

Each took a good stiff drink and moved off, Sparks staggering and Granger hectoring. Both manifested a pretty considerable degree of Dutch courage. The ground was measured, the combatants took their stand, the signal was given. Off went the pistols, when the Doctor brought the knob of his suplejack down on Sparks' head.

'Sparks is shot through the head,' roared Fidler.

'Poz!' exclaimed Doctor Dick, and down dropped Sparks on the ground.

'He's as dead as a door-nail,' said Dickens, 'Escape for your life, Granger; you'll certainly be hung.'

Off scampered Granger as fast as his long legs could carry him down the hill, tumbling head-over heels and picking himself up with incredible alacrity considering he was quite drunk. Sparks was carried into the house and put to bed thinking he was dying fast. Dr Dick tied up his head with cabbage leaves and gave him a huge dose of asafoetida and castor oil, these being about the most nauseous medicines the estate chest could produce.

'Think he'll hold it out till morning, Doctor?' enquired Fidler, pretending to whisper, yet taking care that Sparks should hear.

'He was struck, ye see, Mr Fidler, in a vital part,' answered Dr Dick, speaking softly,

'Has the ball passed through the head, Doctor?' said 'Glass Eye' very feebly.

'It struck yer behind,' said the Doctor, 'and as I can't find any other hole it made, it must jist have taken a kind a slant and come through yer ear, I am athinken Mr Sparks.'

'I felt the ball enter the skull, just as I made a kind of dodge,' said Sparks, 'and then it touched the brain and I fell senseless to the ground. My head is spinning still, Doctor.'

'Grog has much more to do with the spinning, I am afraid,' said Jackson.

'Sparks, ye shoved your head in the way of the ball.'[29]

An athletic planter, overseer on one of the Tharp properties, of the name of Galimore, led the way. Holding on to the withes or scrambling up by roots of trees or low brushwood, with his musket slung across his back by a strong belt of leather, he at length reached a shelving rock on which he took footing and awaited the arrival of the others. In a short time, the Maroon's well-known horn was heard to sound and, the next moment, a rifle-ball stretched Galimore, the gallant leader of the little band, on the ground. His comrades soon surrounded him.

'He's wounded!' exclaimed Jock Mowatt, tying an handkerchief across a wound in the side from which the blood issued fearfully.

'Hello! Galimore,' said Granger, 'are you much hurt?'

'A little more air,' said the wounded man, faintly.

'Good Heavens!' exclaimed Ball.

'He is dying. Poor fellow, to die by the hand of a black savage.'

'Dying, D-y-i-n-g, B-a-l-l,' said the wounded soldier.

'Raise him up,' said Granger, 'and let him take a sup of this,' producing a flask of spirits.

Galimore was raised up to a sitting position and the flask applied to his lips but it was all over. They laid him down; there was a slight gurgling sound, and the soldier was dead.

'What shall we do, Sergeant?' enquired Granger; 'pursue our way, or retreat?'

'Forward, I suppose,' said Sergeant. 'Which of you here can climb best?

'I am a cursed bad climber,' said Granger.

'I can't climb at all,' said Mowatt, 'a prickle has run into my leg.'

'You'd best lead the way, Sergeant,' said Ball.

'I am thinking 'twill be dark before we gain the mountain top,' replied Sergeant Spy, 'and when we're there, what the devil can a handful of men do against a band of armed ruffians, who fire a dozen shots before they are seen once?'

'Tis clear,' said Ball, 'those hypocritical devils of Maroons are siding with the runaways and any of them can put out a candle with a bullet.'

'They have bush tied around them and are standing like the stumps of trees against the huge rocks, and behind them and they are in the clefts and in the thick trees. What can we do with such an enemy as this? In the dark, too, they hear every word we are saying.'

A discharge of rifles here stopped the confabulations and half a dozen bullets whizzed over the volunteers' heads, notes of warning. The men agreed to return to their main body which remained under arms in the gloomy defile which stretched below; not above twenty had been able to scramble up the track where Galimore had led.

'The only man among us who knew anything of the track has been shot, Colonel,' said the Sergeant; 'the pass is like that of Thermopalae, a dozen Maroons with rifles would defend it against our whole force.'

'Just what I have heard, and what I thought,' replied the Colonel. 'Is the private mortally wounded?'

'He is dead,' replied Sergeant Spy. 'The shot was from a Maroon; I know by its deadly aim, besides, we heard their horn.'

'Are we contending, then, with the Maroons?' enquired Major Burn.

'I thought the Maroons were acting in concert with us. If they become leagued with the runaways we shall have some trouble.'

'They are part and parcel of each other as inseparable as body and shadow,' replied the Colonel.

'What's to become of the private's body?' asked the Major. 'Think we'd better have it sent back to headquarters to be interred. The fellow fell bravely and his memory should be treated with due respect.'

'Certainly,' answered the Colonel.

'Order a trooper to ride back to headquarters, and request that half a dozen negroes be sent with a litter to take the body of the brave fellow back to Wales.'

'I think,' said Major Bum, 'if we wish to accomplish our purpose, you had better enquire if any of the officers know the road that leads under the brow of the mountain.'

A cavalry officer rode up.

'Will you undertake, Mr McGuin, to lead us round the hill?' enquired the Colonel.

'I have a negro, Colonel,' replied McGuin, 'who knows every inch of the road as well as I know the way to my dining room – if you will venture to trust him.'

'I think that would be rather hazardous,' answered the commander. 'What do you think, Major?'

'I think at the point of the bayonet he may be trusted. At all events I don't see we shall run any very great risk. If the fellow plays any tricks, of course, we'll hang him up as we shall a score of his comrades to-morrow.'

The negro was placed in front between two soldiers with fixed bayonets and the detachment moved on. They marched, or rather scrambled, along for more than two hours when they came to the foot of a mountain apparently inaccessible.

'Where is the road?' enquired his guards.

'Road lay before you, massa,' answered the slave.

'You are a lying rascal,' said the Major, riding up. 'This is not the road, and you know it very well.'

'No tadder road da, Massa, 'sepen de one you lef' behine,' replied the negro.

'If you don't show the right road you villain, I'll shoot you,' said the Major, drawing a pistol from his holster.

'Two time me come yah,' said the negro, 'dar de way me walk go. If massa will walk follow me, me WE carry him trough, but him we tired 'fore him reach, causin de pass fur. No horse can walk go dey; Massa mus' ride foot.'

'Ride foot, you infernal villain!' exclaimed the irascible Major. 'Didn't you say you knew the way, and was I riding foot when you told me that?'

'Tink say Massa would lef' im ho's wen' 'im ketch yah; massa no tan like 'im can climb.'

In spite of themselves, the officers could not refrain from laughing at this last remark made by the negro. The Major's dimensions were not unlike those of the celebrated Jack Falstaff and the bare idea of his climbing was so perfectly ludicrous as to overreach even the old Colonel's gravity.

'And suppose I left my horse and climbed, you limb of Satan, when would we get to the negro town?' enquired the Major.

'Pen 'pon how massa walk. Massa no use to walk foot an' de pass bad fe true,' replied Caesar.

'Answer the question I ask you, or I'll knock your brains out with the handle of the pistol. If we walk as we have been walking since we left the foot of the other hill, when will we reach the place?' said the Major, speaking as fast as an angry man could.

'Maybe say 'bout fus cock-crow, massa,' replied the guide.

'Midnight! Do you suppose we are going to trust you to carry us into the woods at night?'

'Me tell massa say pass far, massa better tan yah to-night, so wait fe day. If massa please yerry wah me say, 'im won go in ar bush to-night. Plenty yallah snake in dey, an' gallawasp,' answered Caesar.

The Colonel, being in a poor state of health, here resigned his command to Major Burn and returned to headquarters and the men began preparations by order of their commander to bivouac for the night, as it was clearly impossible to scale the mountain and thread out the winding trackless path after night fall, to say nothing of the snakes or gallawasps. Fires were lit and provender spread out and, as there was nothing to fear, the men, fatigued with their march, prepared to rest as best they could, sentries having been posted *pro forma*. Before midnight, silence reigned through every part of the camp. The loud song and boisterous mirth of the soldiers, the talk and giggle of the negro slaves who acted as pioneers had been hushed in slumber; and even the sentries, seated on some stump, or projecting ledges of rock, nodded away their hours of watch. But there was one who neither slept nor slumbered but who, with the eye of a lynx, watched his opportunity. It was Caesar, the negro guide. This man had been for some time in communication with the inhabitants of the runaways' town which was named 'We no Call, You no Come'. By ingratiating himself into the good graces of the white people by giving information, every word of which was false, relative to the situation, extent, population, etc., of the settlement, he was regarded as an enemy to his race and had an opportunity of then becoming acquainted with the movements intended to be made; the night before the troops marched, Caesar had placed the runaways and Maroons in possession of full particulars connected with the attack and, in consequence, a Maroon covered completely with bush which was tied around him was placed in a position to defend the only track that led over the Alpine rocks on the leeward side of the town. This track led immediately through the Maroon encampment, and it is said that no white man ever passed the fatal shelf of rock where Galimore fell. Caesar, who had fallen into the rear with the rest of the slaves that followed as pioneers, retired from his companions as soon as he was convinced they were asleep and, ascending the mountain by a well-known track, reached the town in less then two hours. At the suburb, Caesar was met by Pompey – not like his renowned namesake of old with a numerous army to contend for the rights of a mighty nation, but only with his companions, 'Three-Finger-Jack' – to learn particulars relative to the enemy's approach.

'Which way you'll bring dem come?' enquired Pompey.

'Dat we pen pon de side you goin to sen de woman dem. If me bring dem up John Crow cliff, may be say dem we ketch de gals and de pickney dat jus cum mongst we. Dem know de place can go in big mountain cave no bokarah can eber fine somebody da.'

'Dem hab dog?' asked Three-Finger-Jack.

'No! me no tell you say me pisin obey bit a de dog night afore last,' replied Caesar.

'Den de woman and pickney can go in big-mountain; we bun all the provision, dem won' get noten to nyam and dem can't tan yah no time widout bittle. Breadkind and water nuff da dar de back cave,' said Three-Finger-Jack.

'Berry well,' said Pompey, who appeared to have been considering the best plan of retreat, 'bring dem round Bull Head, and mek 'im fool like you do las' night, bout de snake an gallawasp.'

'You been yerry me wen me da boozle 'im down ar Dead Man Valley?' asked Caesar. 'Hi! you is a clebar nega yar.'

'Me an Tree-Finger no follow you de whole a de pass long de hill-side tell you 'top an de big bokarah draw pistol 'pon you. We could a shoot all de bokarah war ride, easy as me can shoot you now but no use, only mek dem wusser piteful pon dem poo'ting lef dem pon de property. No, time fe fight de right no come yet.'

Then these [negroes][30] descended quietly to the camp and succeeded in stealing and taking away several demijohns of spirits, a dozen stands of arms and a huge bag of bread. With this booty, they returned to the town and began preparations for their evacuation while Caesar, after having taken two or three swigs of grog, stretched himself out among his companions, fully satisfied with the success of his manoeuvres, and he was found fast asleep when called by his master at sun-rise.

Breakfast among soldiers, whether regular troops or militia, is generally settled by a kind of 'summary process'. So it was on this occasion, and the men were under arms at an early hour. The immaculate Caesar, having undergone a very scrutinizing examination by the fat Major who swore that if he manifested the least inclination to escape or unwillingness to proceed in the most direct way to Runaway-Town he would chop off his head with the sword, was once more appointed guide and 'led the forces on'.

Slowly they moved up the precipitous face of the steep, craggy mountain stumbling over roots, stones, logs or withes that grew along the ground. Caesar having led them not only by the most circuitous route, but through the very thickest part of the jungle. Presently, the sun, which they had occasionally caught a glance of, became entirely obscured by dark, heavy clouds, the thunder roared and the lightning flashed fearfully round. The huge caves in the hills echoed back the sound, the wind whistled and the forests and mountains seemed to tremble while huge trees, torn rudely from their widely spreading roots, fell at intervals with an awful crash; the rain-bird screamed out his discordant note from every bush and the crows flew by hundreds over their heads. And now the overcharged dense clouds emptied themselves in a torrent of rain peculiar to tropical countries and especially to mountainous regions, the thunder continuing to roar and the forked streaks of lightning to flash all the time. At length, the wind only whispered among the trees, the thunder ceased to roll and the rain to fall as suddenly as it had commenced; the sun shone forth with his usual splendor, and nothing was heard save the warbling of the mountain birds and the gurgling of the water as it rolled over the precipitous rocks. The clayey ground, now saturated by the rain, became so slippery that it was hardly possible to maintain a footing and there was consequently a great deal of 'lofty stumbling' and literally rolling in the mire. Major Burn seemed to suffer peculiar hardships – caused, no doubt, by the weight of his body, the shortness of his legs, which rendered him incapable of gymnastic exercises and the irascible nature of his temper. At length, having fallen and spoilt his clothes and bruised his skin, his stock of patience, which had been dribbling out in Sunday speeches and prayers during the thunder-storm, seemed to have become entirely exhausted and, he seized Caesar by the throat ...[and]... inflicted such heavy blows on his head with the huge stick with which he walked that the poor fellow roared amain, much to the amusement of the officers and men, who gathered around. Having thus vented his spleen on the negro guide and taken a dram of brandy from Captain Mowatt's flask, the fat commander moved on at a limping pace and, about mid-day, caught the long anticipated sight of 'Me no Call, You no Come'. Here, he hastily drew his men up in battle array and precipitously marched forward. This town, village, hamlet, or collection of huts, as the reader pleases, was situated on a plain in the fastnesses of the forest. They were twenty-three in number, all with thatched roof and one storey, except a building in the centre which seemed to be kept for the transaction of public business and, perhaps, answered the purpose of a chapel on Sunday. In the vicinity, there had been extensive provision grounds; these had been destroyed. At least, everything that had been fit for food had been rooted out. The town had been evacuated and nothing remained besides the empty huts. Here, it was determined to remain at least for the night, and the troops began to make such arrangements for their comfort as circumstances would allow. They now found out what Caesar knew long before, viz., that their stock of bread and spirits and other stores was missing. After another uncomfortable night passed in the woods, everything that would ignite was burnt to the ground and the troops began their retreat early next day, their expedition proving, if not as ridiculous and futile, at least as unsuccessful as Calligula's doughty invasion against the Britons. At headquarters, the regiment dispersed, after having been duly complimented on their military prowess, and informed by their gallant commander that 'the country thanked them for their services'.

Mr Fleming … had resigned his attorneyship in Trelawny …[and]… some material alterations had taken place in the economy of Greenside since our last reference to that estate. Jackson had been discharged by the new attorney. Vernon had sailed for England, accompanied by old Mrs Christy and her protégé, Celeste, the attorney's daughter. Our next chapter will be devoted to Catherine Brown, the fugitive, and Mary Ann who has of late fallen rather into the shade.

Chapter

NINE

*W*hen the weather-beaten pilot ran the good ship Clara so dexterously through the triangles, as mentioned in a former chapter, Catherine was sitting in a disconsolate state of mind on the deck with her eyes riveted on the land from which the vessel was fast receding. She felt isolated in a crowd and seemed, as it were, to stand alone in the world. Her thoughts, in spite of herself, wandered over sea and land and fixed themselves on her aged mother and her Aunt Downey. She could imagine that she heard their expressions of surprise, and saw the distress, which they would ultimately suffer, when months should elapse and no tidings reach them from any of the usual haunts of the fugitives. She thought, too, of Jackson, for she had loved him and, the flame of love once lit up in woman's heart, never expires. It is not to be blunted by indifference, nor chilled by pride, nor wasted by time. This 'love never faileth'; and now it appeared to her that with her own hand she had severed, forever, the link that lately bound her so closely to those she loved, and had spontaneously cast in her lot among strangers. Should these prove unfaithful, where then was her remedy? The next day she took her child on deck and bright visions rose in her mind; she anticipated the day when she should fold it in her arms and call it her own and when she herself should be able to afford it the protection of a mother. But Catherine's gloomy thoughts and brilliant visions were alike chased away by the presence of her mistress, who, in the kindest manner, showed her the way to her cabin and, taking her infant from her arms, laid it herself to sleep.

The homeward passage proved exceedingly pleasant. In a short time, Catherine had become quite a favourite among the lady passengers and, before she reached England, stood high in the estimation of Mrs Arnold. Her native simplicity was interesting and her simple questions very amusing. A young lady of decided religious principles, took much pains in

Catherine's instruction and, before the passage was over, she could spell and read.

At length, the vessel reached her destination, and Catherine's bright vision was fully realized. She embraced her child and for the first time could call it her own, and she herself stood forth, no longer a mere thing but a subject, enjoying, in common, the blessings of the British constitution.

Mrs Arnold treated her with the greatest kindness and paid much attention to her child, until that lady at last fell a victim to a dread complaint; and such was her affection for Catherine that she bequeathed her a hundred pounds as well as her wearing apparel. Poor Catherine felt the loss of her mistress sadly and, once again, she seemed alone in the [world]. But in the order of Divine Providence, her good old friend Mrs Christy arrived in England a fortnight after Mrs Arnold's decease and immediately sent for Catherine to her house. She was treated like a daughter, enjoyed the privileges of a friend, was greatly beloved by Celeste and had the pleasure of seeing Mr Vernon in the midst of his family. But here, for the present, we must leave Catherine Brown to pay some attention to Mary Ann.

The changes that had occurred since the resignation of Mr Fleming, led to a change also in Waldy's affairs which removed him into another employ at a distance from Greenside, and consequently from Mary Ann, who, our readers are aware, form a piece and parcel of that estate. This unhappy girl not only suffered by the absence of Mass George but by the rules of the new overseers; for now if she left the estate on Saturday evening, she was under the necessity of returning early on Monday morning. This limited portion of time little more than sufficed to take her to Wales estate, Waldy's new sphere of labour and to bring her back. Besides, the new Busha was a tyrant and she was often confined and spent her day in the stocks. But there was another circumstance which wrought on poor Mary Ann's feelings more powerfully than either of the foregoing because it touched upon a tender part; it was a report that had reached her in rather an oblique manner, and which reflected on the faithfulness of Mass George. Among the house girls on [the] Wales estate, there was one called Jannett who had, it was said, taken advantage of 'leap year and women's privileges'. True it was that Waldy had not made it appear as clearly as he should have done, in the first instance, that he was 'a married man' and, at best, had offered only a negative resistance to the assaults that were made on his conjugal affection. But, as it is not the customary thing for men in these matters to stand on the defensive, Mass George was not as culpable as at the first blush it might appear, especially as Mary Ann herself ultimately declared that she believed 'de pussen dat tell sech a ting was a liard'.[31]

The joys which Saturday night brings with it to the labouring classes have not diminished since Burns sung its praises. *Certes*, no one ever contemplated its return more ardently than did Mary Ann. On that welcome night she would be seen tripping along, gaily dressed with a small tray on her head, containing Sunday presents for Mass George, singing some scraps of 'negro song' at the pitch of her voice as she passed through the paths that were most dismal on the road. The night had far advanced before Mary Ann reached Wales estate. Late as it was, the house girls were sitting about the stairs talking and looking out into the bright moonlight. As Busha had not yet returned from his evening's visit, they dared not leave their post. Mary Ann walked modestly up and enquired in an undertone for Mr Waldy.

'Oh! a so agen,' replied Jannett, 'spose, mam, you is Mr Waldy lady?'

'Yes, mam, I is de pussen stop wid Mr Waldy,' replied Mary Ann.

'Den 'spose mam, you is anodder one,' said one of the others. 'Mme yare 'bout you.' [32]

'Me don't see de cashun fe all dis, cause me ax fe Mr Waldy,' replied Mary Ann.

'You name, if you please, mam,' said one of the girls.

'Me name Mary Ann Peach,' said Mary Ann.

'Den Miss Mary Ann, me beg pardon – Miss Beech, as I should a said – who is you lef to mine de new Busha, to-night?' asked Jannett.

This imputation was too much for Mary Ann's endurance and, turning on her heel, she exclaimed, 'You is a set of ill-begotten gals,' and forthwith marched towards the kitchen.

'Aunty, can please tell me if Mr Waldy at home?' said Mary Ann, addressing the cook.

The old cook who had a great predilection for tobacco, sat smoking in a kind of drowsy mood over a mass of smouldering coals, near which was carefully placed some roasted roots which were, or had been, intended for Busha's supper. On hearing Mary Ann's salutation she roused herself up and exclaimed:

'Who you?'

'Tis me, mam. I is come from Greenside to see Mr Waldy. Aunty can please show me way him top.'

'Hi, me pickney gall, you da walk sich hours as dis in de King road, 'spose say anybody disturbance you?' said the cook.

'De Almighty is good and grate, aunty, me no feard,' replied Mary Ann.

'But it ain't right. 'Tis sartin me pickney, de Almighty is fren to de po, but a high colour gal like you don' ought to do no sich ting. Me hab mulatta pickney meself, dat's why I bise you, me chile,' said the cook.

'You 'vice is bery good, aunty, but me can't help walk a night time fe me Busha is 'piteful and mek me work late ebryday,' said Mary Ann.[33]

'You must tek care a yousel den,' advised the cook. 'Tek something fe nyam, you mus'e hungry.'

'No a-tenk you, aunty; me beg you fe tek me a Mr Waldy,' entreated Mary Ann.

'Follow me, me chile, an me will show you de way,' said the old woman.

They had not proceeded twenty yards before they met two horsemen.

'Who are you, going there?' asked one of the riders in a loud voice.

'Dar me Busha,' replied the cook, 'an a young gal blangxt to Greenside, Mr Walda sweet-heart.'

'Oh! ho! That's you, Mary Ann, you baggage, there's a nice gal to come all this way after such a rough stick!' exclaimed Waldy.

'Why didn't you stop at the house my girl? I should have been glad to see you' said Mr Stewart, the overseer. 'You must come and see me one of these days when Mr Waldy knows nothing about it.'

'De gals dey good as buse me, Busha. Me couldn't tan dey and put up we dem imprance.' answered Mary Ann.

'Well, come along with us and I'll give you a glass of wine, it'll do you good after your walk.'

The party went up to the overseer's house.

'What right had any of you to illtreat this girl?' said Mr Stewart. And he laid his riding whip right and left over the house girls who scampered away while he sent after them a volley of oaths and hard names, laying great stress on two, the initial letters of which stand nearly at the extremities of the alphabet. Mary Ann was regaled with gingered wine and offered supper by Busha who declared that not one of the Wales girls could touch her by a long pole.

When Mary Ann found herself installed in Waldy's quarters, she began to pour forth her complaints.

'Me yerrie say, Mr Waldy, you no care 'bout me agen.'

'What does that mean in plain English?' asked Waldy.

'Pussen tell me say nodder gal dey lib we you,' said Mary Ann.

'When you see the person,' returned Waldy, 'you can give them my compliments, and tell them to mind their own business.' [34]

'Well, Mass George, if it so you can tell me one time, cause de pass from Greenside ketch yah, is too fur for me to walk for nutten.' said Mary Ann.

'Now, Mary Ann, you are a sensible girl, you mustn't let people trouble you with idle stories. You are my only girl and you know I am too fond of you to trouble my head about another.'

'Tink say you ben promise to buy me, den I can top wid you all [de] time, and wait 'pon you. Mass George, you can't write ask Massa a England?' enquired Mary Ann.

'Mr Vernon wrote to tell me that Mr Cunningham won't sell any of his slaves unless to themselves. If you are not to be free, he says, you might as well belong to him, for he treats you all kindly and I am going to buy you free,' said Waldy.

'Mass George, a fe true you going to buy me free?' enquired Mary Ann very earnestly.

'True, I am going to see the Attorney next week, and I have the money to buy you. Cunningham says if you are to be free he'll sell you cheap. See here, what I have brought for you,' said Waldy displaying a handsome pair of ear-rings and a bunch of corals.

Whatever effect the old story of being bought free had on Mary Ann, [it] is certain the display of these presents proved a peace offering and entirely silenced all further allusion to the subject that had caused her so much uneasiness.[35] So Mary Ann continued her weekly peregrinations with the greatest regularity between Greenside and Wales Estate and [for] a long time, nothing occurred worthy of any particular remark. In spite of Busha's remonstrances, the house girls often made themselves merry at her expense and buxomly sang scraps of songs as she passed within hearing which had reference to her shoes and stockings, her necklace or ear-rings. This, however, was borne with great fortitude by the Greenside girl who had shrewd suspicions that she was an object of envy.

On a certain evening, Mary Ann had been later than usual in leaving Greenside. The night was gloomy and consequently she sang louder than usual. As the negroes believe nothing favours the visits of the 'Duppy' more than silence, they always sing when alone in the dark. Passing through rather a murky valley, her attention was arrested by something white, fearfully white, too white, she was convinced, to be anything good. [It] seemed to spread itself immediately in her path. Her first impression was a retreat, but the idea of giving the 'Duppy' an opportunity of jumping on her shoulders and hugging her to death was too horrid a thought to be for an instant entertained. No, if die she must, she should see when the blow was struck. She now remembered the morsel of advice she had received on her primeval visit to Wales from old Eley, the cook, about late hours, and she racked her brains to recollect if she had ever heard of a murder that had been committed on that spot. To be sure, there had. How could she have been such a fool to pass this place when, by the King's Highway, it was only two miles more to Wales? Linton Park people had once murdered an overseer here and, of course, this must be his duppy. Mary Ann devoutly said the Lord's Prayer and repeated the ten commandments when she observed a horse standing at a distance. True, a horse could promise little for she knew very well that these poor animals themselves were often made to suffer martyrdom by the 'duppies' who rode them unmercifully whenever they had journeys to make at night. Frequently were they seen by nocturnal travellers at full speed with their faces towards the tail, which answered for a bridle. However, drowning men and frightened women alike catch at straw and she approached the animal with the intention of entering into a kind of 'defensive treaty' against the common enemy. Perceiving that he was caparisoned with saddle and bridle, she began to suspect that the object of her dread was not a real 'duppy', but some unhappy rider who had been thrown from his horse. She now approached rather gingerly and made a 'dodge' at his bridle, whereon Rosanante resisted order very buxomly and sent up his heels. This movement Mary Ann considered quite tantamount to a declaration of war and, snatching at the first stick that came to hand, made a charge and triumphantly drove the enemy before her into the path where, after a short siege, she quite conquered him.[36] She now ascertained that the 'white thing' was her old acquaintance, Sparks, who was snoring on the green sward. This gentleman, who had paid very ardent devotions at the shrine of Bacchus during the evening had, thus, been laid low. Indeed, this was not the first time that his adoration of the rosy god had brought him down from a lofty position. All attempts at resuscitation resulting only in kicks and curses, Mary Ann proceeded to the estate on which 'Glass-Eye' did duty as Busha, which happened to be pretty near, and communicated with the domestics on the subject.

As soon as her mission of having Sparks rescued was fulfilled, Mary Ann took a short-cut through the canefields which, she felt sure, would carry her directly to Wales. Instead of going, like the Irishman, 'straight round the corner,' she followed her nose and got completely out of her way .... Quite lost, she saw a light at a distance which she supposed to stream from some watchman's fire. Towards this she eagerly bent her steps. She found the place, from whence the light issued, to be a dilapidated building which, in days of yore, had been used as a receptacle for those negroes among the slaves afflicted with yaws. As this disease is highly infectious, it was necessary that they should be entirely separated from the other slaves, hence the isolated position of this old house.

As she drew near, she heard persons engaged in earnest conversation and immediately recognised the peculiar voice of a Maroon. The girl peered through a crevice and saw some men sitting around a smoky lamp talking excitedly. She turned to go away but, just as she was leaving the spot, she heard someone mention the name of Waldy. Her interest having been awakened, she ventured on a further scrutiny and discovered that one of the three men was Quamin, of whom she had seen nothing since the affair of the dungeon, a slave from Wales and Maroon chief. Their plot, she soon discovered, was an attack on Wales Estate. The provision store was to be plundered; as much sugar and rum carried off as possible; the white men murdered and the estate itself fired. By what she could gather from their conversation, it appeared that there were about twenty Maroons and as many slaves engaged in this conspiracy. The attack was to be made at midnight on the following Saturday, the party assembling in the old house, where they now were, by ten o'clock and from there they would go to the property.

Having gained this information, Mary Ann[37] retraced her steps and, having been directed by a slave she met, found the right track and at last reached her destination. Late as it was when Mary Ann reached Wales, she found her friend Waldy smoking his cigar. When she had placed her little tray on a shelf, she seated herself on a trunk and, placing one of her hands under her chin, leaned her head forward and remained for a while in a kind of brown study. At length she spoke.

'Mass George, me yerry something tonight dat lay heaby pon me heart, but me is feard to 'peak.'

'See duppy, I suppose,' said Waldy, knocking the ashes from his cigar and laughing. I see you are afraid. Come and sit near me.'

The girl drew close up. Waldy patted her cheek and tried to make her look cheerful, but in vain. He kissed her and drew her nearer, but still she seemed to shrink from his caresses and trembled with fear. At length she said:

'Mass George, if me no tell you wha' me yerry, neygar dem will murder you, an' if dem know sa a me tell 'pon dem, da will kill me elsen pisin me, but me no mine. Come inside an' me will tell you.' Waldy now felt some concern and went into the room. Mary Ann, having convinced herself, by ocular demonstration, that no one was playing eavesdropper, related what she had heard that evening. Waldy, after some trouble, convinced the frightened girl that there was not the least occasion for anyone to know that she had discovered the plot and cautioned her to keep the secret to herself while he determined to disclose the affair to the attorney.

Accordingly, next morning he rode over to Good Hope where that individual resided and communicated with him on the subject. With great prudence, the two laid a plot which succeeded in counterchecking the conspiracy. The attorney directed all the white people in the employ to rendevouz at a certain spot, which was central, immediately after dark, on the Saturday following, armed and accoutred. As every white person on the estates was provided with a stand of arms and Saturday was a partial holiday with the planters, and riding about after dark a thing of too ordinary occurrence to excite any attention, these movements were carried out without creating any alarm.

The men, having assembled to the number of twenty-five including the attorney, who placed himself at their head, marched by a circuitous route to the outskirts of the estate and posted themselves in an advantageous position. A few, having been sent to recconoitre in the neighbourhood of the old house, returned and stated that the conspirators had assembled. Shortly after, a small body of men was seen moving stealthily along towards the works. By a peculiar foraging cap, this party was identified as Maroons, and the men in the ambush fired. Only two of the number fell, although no doubt was entertained that many were wounded. Owing, however, to the darkness of the night, together with the thick brushwood in the vicinity, the others effected their escape. One of the captured Maroons died, the other recovered, though he had been very seriously wounded but, notwithstanding the offer of a pardon and other inducements that were held out, he obstinately refused to make any disclosures or to implicate any of the slaves. Quamin was discovered in the old house, quite drunk, and readily confessed all he knew. From this, it appeared that the Maroons had urged on the slaves to aid them in the plot; that the estate was to have been pilfered of everything that was portable and then fired, and that all who offered any opposition were to be murdered. Of the negroes implicated, Quamin knew nothing, at least so he said, having been working for the Maroons since 'duppy frightened him off Greenside'.

When, however, the man whom Mary Ann had seen was mentioned, he reluctantly acknowledged that he had met the Maroons in the old yaws-house on two occasions. The Maroon and the slave were executed and, although there was no tangible proof of the guilt of any of the others, many of the slaves on the estate were punished with great severity. Quamin, faithful to his old office of King's evidence, received a pardon and was restored to his old sphere of labour on Greenside, but always made himself scarce when placed as watchman of the dungeon.

Mary Ann's freedom was purchased for her by the proprietor of Wales, though the slaves always believed that she had been bought free by Waldy.

After residing a few years in England, Mrs Christy returned to Jamaica, bringing Catherine with her. The child, Mr Vernon had placed at school. The day after her arrival, Catherine visited Greenside and Aunt Downey. She had the satisfaction to learn that her mother was well but, much to her grief, could obtain no tidings of Jackson beyond the fact of his having latterly fallen into very indigent circumstances.

Chapter

TEN

*I*t was late on a December evening that a careworn looking, 'Walking Buckra' reached Richmond Estate in the Parish of St Ann. He looked sickly and was shivering with cold. Yes, shivering with cold, for rain, a bleak wind and threadbare habiliments will cause a European to tremble, even beneath a tropical sky. This individual was Jackson.

On leaving Greenside, the discharged overseer had entered into a kind of liquor and grocery business at a village much frequented by seamen as it stretched directly along a fine open bay. Owing however to untoward circumstances, together with a protracted fit of sickness, this business failed. He fell into disrepute with the merchants who had formerly supplied his store and, ultimately, into reduced circumstances. He called on his companion Granger, hoping at least to meet with a warm reception, but his quondam friend evinced unmistakeable signs that his absence was his best company and, in the spirit of a Job's comforter, sympathisingly told him that 'it was his own fault' that he suffered, for had he 'only cut up those rascally lazy niggers and made more sugar, the new attorney never would have sent him about his business as he had'.

Jackson, stung to the quick by these reproaches from a man whom he had served effectually when in reduced circumstances, snatched up his hat and, without uttering a syllable, left the house. On his way from the property he met several of his former acquaintances riding up. As it was about dinner time, he began to think that Granger had a party that day and was anxious to get him out of the way as, in the garb he then wore, he certainly would not have graced a select party of gentlemen at dinner.

Jackson was correct in his surmises. Great preparations had been made at Maxfield for a 'feed' on a grand scale. Fidler, Jack Mowatt, Dr Dick and others of a similar stamp were Granger's favoured guests. As they sat over their glasses after dinner, Mowatt said: 'I saw a fellow walking along with a small bundle in his hand, as I rode up. Blast me, if I didn't think it looked like Jackson.'

You are right,' returned Granger. 'The stupid ass called here and wanted me to help him with a beast to Kingston. I began to give him a little wholesome advice but he got into a high dudgeon and walked off.'

'What will the blockhead do in Kingston? Go to the poor-house, I suppose,' said Fidler.

'Poz!' exclaimed Dr Dick, striking the table with the handle of his knife.

'And yet that was as smart a fellow as the best amongst us,' said Mowatt. 'D—n me if he couldn't a broken a neygar's neck as soon as a taken a glass a punch when I knowed him first.'

'I seen him flog a gal once to such a pitch that he'd to fix her up in the bilboes for upwards of a month for fear she'd go ashowing off herself to one of those infernal new magistrates that's akicking up a devil of a row whenever one of them lose a little skin, as if the black imps were not made to be slaves,' said Granger.

'You have forgot the best part of the story,' said Mowatt. 'The stupid fool give the gal two doubloons to keep dark, and off went the brute and not only showed her hide [which, I am told, was pretty well done up] but the money into the bargain, and that bloody old Methedis', Benjamin, took the case up and Jackson only escaped [by] the skin of his teeth.'

'Had he dressed her back with salt pickle, he'd have cured her soon enough,' said Granger. 'Don't yer think, Doctor, that's a good dressing for a sore hide?'

'Why, Mr Granger, ye see, though I hear some persons say that the negro is a different species to ourselves, I can't say that I ever differ much in my mode of practise when I prescribe. I find my medicines produce the same effect on the negro as on his master. You'll understand me, I hope, Mr Granger. I don't mean to say positively that the negro and the white man are alike as regards either the solids or fluids in the vicera in general. I only speak as to the effects of my medicine on his constitution,' replied Dr Dick.

'I suppose, Doctor, you are a bit of a philosopher?', [asked] Fidler, handing his silver snuff box.

'Why, ye see, Mr Fidler, I've just paid about as much attention to Reed and the other Scotch philosophers as the rest of the faculty. It don't require much philosophy, Mr Fidler, as ye must know, to be an estate doctor,' said Dr Dick, shoving a pinch of snuff into his huge nostrils.

'I wouldn't give a glass of punch for all your philosophy, Doctor,' said Mowatt. 'Come Granger, shove your grog about a little more liberally or we won't be likely to get drunk tonight. Do you know anything of the philosophy of drunkenness, Dr Dick? He! He! He!'

'Jackson is good-hearted fellow, notwithstanding his faults,' said Glass Eye, 'but he broke down after his girl went off.'

'Cussed fool,' replied Granger, 'he used to lick that gal well once, though he wants to back out of it now. Just as he became a little kind to her the d—n jade took herself off. If he had as much sense as a jackass he would have known that so long as she had any d——d black blood in her she couldn't do without the whip. Had he brought her back from the negro houses and given her over to the driver, as I always do with my gal when she puts on any of her airs, he'd a kept her at home, that he would.'

'I always told him she cared as much for the weather-cock stuck on top of the mill-house as she did for him, but he wouldn't believe me. He was always as obstinate as a mule. The fellow has lived to find my word come true though,' said Mowatt, swallowing a glass of punch.

'I hear that grimalkin, Mrs Christy, had a hand in getting that gal off the island,' [remarked] Fidler.

'Yes, and the attorney is trying hard to draw the old hag over the coals, but he can't get the shadow of proof. Not one of her slaves would tell a word against her if you were to flay them alive,' said Granger.

'I wish she was in the pillory,' said Fidler.

'Poz!' said the doctor, nodding his head and striking the table with his fist. 'Her and I don't [gee], Mr Fidler.'

'If I go to hell I think I'll find Dame Christy there, grumming it out,' said Mowatt. 'She got me out of the best berth I ever had because I liked a negro woman "in a family way", as she called it. I only wish I could prove that she helped off Jackson's gal, but we intend to frighten her about the matter. We hear the gal returned to the island under her care.'

'I think the affair of that hypocritical old rascal, Williams, did Jackson more harm than anything else. I don't believe the attorney liked his interfering in the matter,' [commented] Fidler.

'That's sartin, he didn't!' [agreed] Granger.

'Poz!' said the man of physic.

'You are right there, to a notch,' chimed in Mowatt.

'What matter was that?' enquired a bloated-faced planter, answering to the name of Mick who, for the last half hour, had been bargaining with his neighbour about a horse.

'You must have heard of the old Baptist leader they said was flogged to death over at Bold Attempt?' [asked Granger].

'Mick is always so busy bargaining,' said Fidler, winking at the Doctor 'that he wouldn't have time to hear if his mother had died, much less a nigger.'

'Poz,' replied Dr Dick, shoving his glass forward to be replenished and making another attack on the pulverised tobacco.

Let's hear the affair,' said Mick, finishing his tumbler of grog and trying to look composed, though, from his occasional vacant stare, it seemed as if he was calculating whether he was likely to lose or gain in the bargain he had just struck.

'Why, you see,' said Granger, 'that fellow was just as troublesome an old rascal as ever tormented a plantation. He would go from place to place singing Psalms and preaching, as he said, to the negroes at night, keeping them up until a late hour and putting nonsense of all kinds into their heads. He was set on by those d——d missionaries to bring the foolish slaves to their chapels [and] to raise their funds.'

'I hear they are gathering up all the macaronies in the island,' said Fidler, 'I believe the negroes will steal wherever they can to put the money into their box.'

'I say, Chance,' exclaimed Mick, 'does that pony stumble?'

'I never knew him go on his knees in my life,' replied Chance.

'That's just like his master to the life,' said one of the party.

'Nobody ever cursed Michael Noble for a saint, I am certain,' said Mowatt.

'And yet,' replied Mick, appearing not to relish such unenviable notoriety,' when I lived with my ould mother I went regularly to Kirk three times every Sunday and I never used my Maker's name without feeling a kind of reverence, but I am sorry to say that I can scarce now open my mouth without taking His name in vain. However, I hope soon to pocket my winnings and be off again to the old home.'

'No country, Mr Noble,' said the Doctor, 'for morality and religion and all that, like old Scotia. I'm athinkin' should I live to return, I'll go on my knees and kiss the sods. But we have interrupted you, Mr Granger, in your story about the old man.'

'And before he begins again,' said Sparks, 'we must whet our whistle. Granger's stories are always long-winded.'

'Like the pony I've just sold,' said Chance.

Here, there was a long pull, a strong pull and a pull all together and Granger proceeded with the story of Father Williams.

'Why, I say, the stupid old fool, egged on by those hell-brands, went from one estate to another, persuading the people to neglect their provision grounds and go to the chapels on a Sunday. We flogged them infernally hard whenever we found their grounds foul, but all to no purpose, for many of the obstinate devils cleaned their grounds in the moonlight so as to have Sunday to themselves and then we laid hold of the old villain and clapped [h]im in the stocks and starved [h]im for a time, but back he came again in a fortnight after, with his cursed singing and praying as bad as ever. Then we tried the whip, but still the rascal returned. At last, he got over to Bold Attempt and Fraser who, you know, is one of the old time daddies, hates parsons as much as he does lawyers and doctors. He would sooner hear the cry of 'Fire!' any time than psalm singing. So he told the old chap very plainly that if he sang hymns there, he should sing them where Paul and Silas did, and clapped him in the stocks. At night, the old fellow set up such a howling that Fraser went into the dungeon and gave him a rather hard drubbing and, they say, trampled him under his feet. He offered to release him next day if he would promise to return to the estate no more. The old limb of Satan refused to keep away and Fraser had him laid down and severely flogged. After that, he was sent home hand-cuffed and a week later he died. Jackson, like the d——d fool he always was, tells Mitchell that Williams died from the effects of the flogging. This report reaches the ears of that old cat Christy, with her old crooked nose, and she sends up the coroner. Luckily, slave evidence ain't worth nothing or poor Fraser might have been put to a great deal of trouble and expense. Not satisfied with all this fuss about an old worn-out slave that wasn't worth ten pounds, she get Benjamin to write to the Colonial Office, and Miller had the deuce of a trouble to hush the matter up.'

'I think Fraser was wrong to use the blasphemous expressions that he did. It won't sound well in England,' said Dr Dick.

'Why, 'tis true,' said Granger, 'it was going rether far, but ye see Doctor, Fraser hates all religions but his own and he cusses awful when he hears about these canting hypocrites – he loses his temper like.'

'Aye, he always swears he'll never forsake the religion of his forefathers,' remarked Fidler, handing his snuff-box as usual to his friends rather smirkily.

'Religion of his forefathers,' said Mowatt laughingly. 'I wonder what that religion was?'

'They weren't Nazarenes at any rate,' said Mick.

'Poz!' replied the Doctor. 'I see, Mr Noble, ye still retain a smattering of your Biblical knowledge and I am just athinking his ancestors never entered their vote relative to polygamy.'

'Come, Doctor, I know you have an old grudge against Fraser. Ye had a little sparring once, I recollect,' said Fidler. 'Fraser is fond of his glass I allow and equally so of the girls – yet I daresay he never had as many wives as Solomon or King David.'

'That's only because he couldn't get 'em,' said Sparks, who was now half drunk and seemed ready to begin an argument once more with Granger on distillation as he had sniffed twice at the last drink and muttered something about the insufficiency of dunder.

'Poor Jackson, I hope he'll get off to his friends in Scotland. I hear some of them are well-to-do in the world,' said Chance. 'You've seen that gal of his since she returned from her runaway trip, haven't you Granger?'

'Yes, I saw her t'other day in Falmouth. D—n me, if I knew her at first sight. She looks as buxom as you'll wish any gal of seventeen to look and talks as if she had been born a lady,' replied Granger.

'I wonder if she asked after Jackson,' said Mick.

'Not she, indeed, after she heard he'd gone to the dogs, I warrant ye,' replied Jock Mowatt.

Most of the party had begun to manifest signs of being a little 'sprung'. The Doctor took his leave and Granger called on Mowatt for his well-known song of the Methodist Parson (which he sung to the tune of Yankee Doodle):

'Parson Angus had a call
For to gull his cronies;
And when he preached an hour or so
He took their macaronis.

Says he, 'My worthy christian friends
Old Nick's your constant crony,
And all on him, not on the church,
You spend you macaroni.

We servants of the church, the saints,
Have stomachs for polonies,
But how then can we buy this food
If you give not macaronis?

'The Pope is a good fellow,' and severally other songs equally as elegant in composition, if not as moral in their tendency, followed and, at a late hour, some of the party found their way to bed whilst others satisfied themselves with one of the softest benches.

ELEVEN

A short time after Mrs Christy's return from England, while at breakfast one morning, she was informed that a gentleman desired to speak to her on business. Our 'old lady' was not one of ordinary stamp. Nobody ever heard her complain of weak nerves and, had the house been falling about her ears, she would have called 'Bunchy', to tell her what was the matter before she moved out of her huge old-fashioned arm-chair, stuffed with horse hair and lined with Morocco. No, no, Mrs Christy never had been heard to say, 'I thought I should have died.' She knew what everybody knows very well, that any life insurance office would sooner have one 'old lady' on their books than half-a-dozen young ones. Besides, Mrs Christy was an annuitant and, who ever heard of an 'old lady' with an annuity dying? Had a lighted candle been stuck on the edge of a keg of gunpowder, Mrs Christy would have taken it off without evincing any fear. No wonder, then, that she desired the gentleman to be shown into the breakfast room, without manifesting any curiosity about his business at such an unbusinesslike time of day. There, the old lady sat at the head of her breakfast table, looking just as prim as she had done ten years before, every ruffle, every pin just where 'Bunchy' had placed it when she dressed her at five o'clock for her morning's walk. Her bright tea-kettle stood at her right hand and the handsome tortoiseshell tea-caddy, received as a wedding present, at her left. Between these extremities, there was a set of real old china in a japanned tray with toast and eggs. Having desired the gentleman to take a seat, she leisurely concluded her morning's repast, occasionally asking a commonplace question. At length, she rose and inviting the stranger into her drawing room, entered into business. Her guest was Clerk of the Peace for the parish.

'I have been instructed by the attorney of Mr Cunningham, Madam, to wait on you in reference to a slave said to be harboured by you from Greenside.'

'Said to be harboured by me? Can you inform me, sir, who said it?' asked Mrs Christy.

'I was told – at least, Mr Nelson said – it was a common report, Mrs Christy,' answered the man of law.

'Common reports are not always true, Mr Clerk of the Peace,' replied the old lady.

'Then I am to understand that you deny the accusation, Madam,' said the peace officer.

'I neither deny, sir, nor affirm. There will be quite time for that when I learn who my accuser, or accusers are,' answered Mrs Christy.

'Good morning, Madam,' said the parish officer.

'Good morning, sir,' returned Mrs Christy.

In the course of the day, our aged friend received a visit from another legal functionary, accompanied by the attorney for Greenside.

'We have been authorised, Madam, by His Honour the Custos to call on you to enquire if you know any particulars respecting a slave belonging to Greenside estate ...'

'By the name of Williams, that was murdered at 'Bold Attempt' in the most ...', [interjected Mrs Christie].

'No, Madam, you are mistaken in ...'

'I suppose, sir, in speaking of that slave, I am, to use legal phraseology, travelling beyond the record.'

'Our object, Madam, in visiting you, is to enquire if you know anything about a woman called Catherine Brown.'

'I know, sir, that Catherine Brown resided in England for more than two years; that previously to her return to this country she procured the Lord Mayor's certificate of this fact,' replied Mrs Christy.

'I tell you what, old lady,' said the attorney almost choked by rage, 'you are accused of having inveigled that girl to leave the estate. Of this we have proof.'

'Has the act, sir, prohibiting slave evidence, been lately disallowed?' enquired Mrs Christy.

'It is not because you have been fool enough to give your own slaves free[dom] that you are justified in aiding to defraud other persons of their property,' said the attorney.

'If you address me again, sir, in that strain or tone of voice, I shall be under the necessity of ordering my servants to expel you from my premises,' replied Mrs Christy.

'Expel a gentleman acting under sanction of [the] law? Besides, Madam, do you know that you have the honour of addressing the attorney for all Cunningham's properties?' said the lawyer.

'The prince of the slave drivers then, I suppose. And I presume that you, sir, are the King of the Cannibal Islands,' answered the old lady.

'I will find means, Madam, of making you know that I am Defender of Slaves according to law!' exclaimed the legal functionary.

'And I, Sir, embrace the present opportunity of informing you, and through you all others whom it may concern, that I am defender of slaves according to the gospel. Our business, at least for the present, is at an end. Here, Jasper, show these gentlemen out,' said our old friend.

'Are we to consider ourselves expelled Madam?' enquired the law officer.

'Certainly,' replied Mrs Christy, 'expelled for impertinence.'

The attorney of estates and his legal friend were shown out by the black butler, and no further attempts were made to 'frighten' old Mrs Christy.

But it is now time to return to Jackson. On his abruptly parting with Granger, he determined to make no further experiments on the hospitality of his other friends, but to proceed to Kingston, the only port in the island where there was any certainty of finding a trans-atlantic vessel at that time of the year, and endeavouring to obtain a steerage passage for fifteen or thirty pounds, this sum being all that his coffers were found to contain when he wound up his mercantile transactions and struck his balance sheet. In the prosecution of this plan, as we stated in another page, he reached Richmond, in St Ann's where he received 'second class' entertainment for the night and resumed his journey at an early hour next morning.

Catherine, having ascertained from her mother in the mountains, on whom Jackson had called, that he had left Trelawny for Kingston, resolved to trace him out. Mrs Christy had for a time opposed her resolves on the subject but, finding that the poor woman seemed really miserable, she at length withdrew her opposition. She felt convinced that Catherine would act with prudence in the matter and thought that the bare attempt, even if unsuccessful, would palliate the fever of her mind. Having been provided with a good saddle-horse and a trusty female servant, who walked, carrying a tin case on her head, Catherine started with a hope almost as forlorn as that of the expeditions sent in search of the lamented Franklin.

Many were the enquiries made both by Mistress and servant, as they proceeded, at lonely houses or petty shops, standing so directly by the high road as to invite the travellers in a sultry clime to ask for a cup of cold water or shelter from a drenching shower. As it was a most uncommon thing for any other persons than slaves to walk, it was derogatory in the highest degree for white persons to be pedestrians.

A 'walk-foot buckra', in the negro's eye, was everything that was mean and pitiful. Consequently, they were well remembered months after they passed, by those who met them on the way. No definite information, however, was received until our traveller and servant reached a wharf some time after noon. The watchman stated that a buckra had called at his hut to escape the rain and that he had advised him not to call at the estate to which the wharf belonged 'as Busha neber treat somebody good dat ride foot go da', but go to Richmond, the estate further on. Poor Catherine drank in every word that the old man said without being able to identify the person as Jackson. At length, the old fellow rather reluctantly confessed that he buckra had 'forget his handkercher', but lest this admission should result in the loss of the aforesaid article, the informant had some fears that it could not be forthcoming, to wit, he had given it to his wife and 'she mus'a loss'e'. To a promise of remuneration, the old man appeared sceptical, but ocular and palpable demonstration was a rather undisputable kind of evidence and the worthy guardian of the wharf immediately started on an experimental trip and, shortly after, the wife and handkerchief simultaneously made their appearance. With the former, Catherine at once entered into terms of friendship and alliance and felt convinced that she had been on similar terms with the latter long before. On this point there could be no mistake, as the letters had been worked on it by her own hand at a time, too, when her literary attainments were so far below mediocrity that two of them were inverted, owing simply to her having placed the book from which she copied part of the time upside down. Matters having been adjusted so as to afford mutual satisfaction, the Busha's Mistress proceeded to Richmond.

Since Jackson had passed on his weary pilgrimage to Kingston; Challener, who was overseer when Jackson called, had been politely discharged by his Attorney, Charley Smith, why or wherefore 'deponent doth not further declare'; and Fidler, of silver snuff-box notoriety, had, through the interest of a relative, been exalted from a paltry estate in Trelawny to this large flourishing estate in St Ann's, the only one perhaps in the island overlit by gas. As it was not an ordinary thing for respectable looking females to visit estates, Catherine's appearance excited some interest. The old cook peeped carefully from the crevice of the kitchen door, the house girls from the half-closed pantry window, while a host of ragged urchins ran off as fast as their legs could carry them. At length an old man who had been carrying a couple of wretched-looking hacks, [met them] at the stable gate. His employment had evidently answered as a sudorific, for he rubbed away at his face and neck almost as hard as he had done at the hairy old nags. Though this 'old boy' was ignorant of the Book of Genesis, he was painfully aware of the fact that 'he was doomed to get his bread by the sweat of his brow'. In no very good humour he approached the house and began to roar to Thomas 'to holla to James to come and tell Robert to tell Busha that somany want 'im up yah'.

At length, this message having reached the overseer's ears, he came up to the house.

'Bless my stars,' exclaimed Fidler on seeing Catherine, 'am I dreaming? Isn't this Jackson's gal? Ain't your name Catherine Brown?'

'Yes,' replied Catherine. 'I am the person you take me for. I am on my way to Kingston. I suppose Miss Lyon will give me and the person with me a lodging to-night.'

'Why, Catherine, I always thought you a nice girl, and you are so much improved since I knew you at Greenside that I would be very glad to help you in any way, but I am afraid I might get into a trouble. You know there is a very heavy penalty for harbouring slaves.'

'But you know, Mr Fidler, I am not a slave now. Nobody can be a slave that has once been to England.'

'But, my girl,' said Fidler, 'who taught you to speak so well? I never saw anybody so much changed in the course of a few years. At all events,' he continued, 'come in and get something to eat.'

She went in and took a seat in the piazza and Fidler summoned Miss Lyon, who soon made her appearance, and, recognizing Catherine, gave her a kind of 'maternal hug', she having been a playmate, as she said, of her mother's.

'Did you ever see a girl so much altered as she is, Eliza, in all your life?' asked Fidler.

'Me wouldn't a-know em agin if me been meet em any way, but jis em peak, me tink say me know de bice. Catran is a cleber gal, em raley do de ting cunning,' said Miss Lyon.

'Then you think she was quite right in running away and getting herself free, do you? And you encourage her in her tricks,' said Fidler.

'For sartin, de gal is right,' returned Miss Lyon. 'Ah, say, Mass Jim, 'pose say dem mek you slave, you would tan put up wid 'buse, and whip, and box all time? You no would try fe get 'way?'

'Well, Eliza, I suppose I would, but people that are born slaves don't feel it as I should,' replied Fidler.

'I wish say me could fine any pussen dat would carry me go dah England, mek me free like a Catran. Hi! me would a glad. A say, cousin, war you do we Jimbo?' quoth Miss Lyon.

'I have left the little boy in England to be sent to school,' replied Catherine.

'God bless you me chile, you do berry well. Me would sooner see Tommy bury dan him should carry 'way from me, an' me neber so much as to know wa' him da so-so,' said Miss Lyon, wiping the corner of her eyes with her check apron.

'Well, Catherine, you can stop with Eliza to-night, but you mustn't tell anybody that I harboured you or I'll get into a hobble, I suspect.' On saying this the overseer left the house.

When he was gone Catherine comforted Miss Lyon very much about Tommy by telling her of the efforts that were being made in England for the abolition of slavery and that she was sure the slaves would all be free before Tommy could be taken away from her.

'But Catran,' enquired Miss Lyon, 'how you come to larn to 'peak so pretty? Dem teach you book a Englan?'

'All the ladies that I stop't with taught me something. All were good to me, but one young miss made me read and write three times every day, and I used to sit up late at night to learn the lessons she gave me,' replied Catherine.

'Den, Catran,' enquired Miss Lyon 'you can write letter? Englan' mus' be a wanderful place fe true!'

'Oh, yes,' replied Catherine, 'I can write a letter, but not very well, but I am still learning with the big Misses?'

'An' den, Catran, you goin to tek up we Mr Jackson agen, as 'im sweetheart, 'pose you fine 'im a-town?' asked Miss Lyon.

'On no account,' replied Catherine. 'By God's mercy, I have been brought to see that the way in which I lived was disgraceful and sinful and it would be a greater sin now for me to return to such a state of life than it was before to remain in it. When I was a slave, I was afraid of the cruel treatment I saw others suffer who refused to lead such lives. I was always dreadfully afraid of the Dungeon and I never knew then that the Almighty cared anything about negroes. I thought His curse had made them black and made them slaves and only white people could ever get to Heaven, and that as we had so much trouble in this world we never should be punished again in the next world, but now ...'

'Den, Catran,' said her companion interrupting, ''tis de Almighty mek we all slabe?'

'No,' replied Catherine. 'The ladies all told me it was a sin that the negroes were kept in slavery, that God loved black and white just alike if they were good, and they said that the time would come when all would be free alike, and now I can read the Bible myself I see that God is good to all, and that the Saviour, Jesus Christ, died for all men.'

'Den you tink say if me pray 'bout Tommy, de Almighty will yerrie wah me say?' asked Miss Lyon.

'Of Course, God will hear anyone that prays, but you must pray for yourself, Eliza, for we are all sinners and we shall be lost if we do not pray,' returned Catherine.

'After I living in sich a way of sin, Catran, how I is to pray? Don't de minister tell we say to lib we anybody widout we is married is sin?' asked Miss Lyon.

'That is the reason,' said Catherine, 'that I told you I couldn't think of living in that way again, and you must leave it off.'

'How I is to leave Mass Jim? Dis ten years me is libing we 'im an' if me lef 'im wah goin to become of Tommy? Me no care so much bout myself,' said Miss Lyon, very sadly.

'You must leave that to God. Pray constantly to Him and He will help you. It would be hard, I know, for you to leave Mr Fidler but the Almighty can bring things to pass in a way that we never could think of.'

A great deal more conversation of a similar kind took place between Catherine and her old friend Eliza Lyon. Catherine told her that her intentions were to rescue Jackson from what she feared would be ruin. Mrs Christy had promised to use her interest to procure him a situation and she had a little money with which she could help him.

'Had he been in good circumstances,' said Catherine, 'I should not have gone to look after him, but as it is, I am willing to suffer any hardship if I can but see him again in a decent situation. Perhaps had I remained with him, he would never have come to what he has.'

Early the following morning Catherine and her trusty servant proceeded on their journey and on that night rested at a tavern at the foot of the well-known 'Devil's Mountain'. The sun rose the next morning as they ascended the hill and sunk into darkness as they reached Spanish

Town, the old Spanish capital of the island. The day following, they arrived in Kingston.

Nothing could well exceed the bustle that existed in this busy city. Carriages, gigs, carts, and drays, drove furiously along the streets. Here, gentlemen were hurrying forward in one direction, there, ladies walked leisurely in another. There were boys and girls admiring the curiosities that dazzled in the windows of the variety shops while others, with books and slates, were making the best of their way to or from their schools. Slaves, linked together with huge iron chains and collars, were pulling along carts filled with rubbish, and others with long brooms of birch swept the streets, or moved wearily along, bearing heavy burdens on their heads while a host of pedlars roared out something which nobody even pretended to understand.

Poor Catherine's heart sickened as she rode amidst all this hurryscurry and thought how slender her chance was of meeting with Jackson. She passed through the Parade, paying little attention to the handsome buildings which ornament the square nor to the imposing uniform and bright armour of the soldiers who were parading. Forward she went, up one street and down another until, at length, her servant stopped at a small house in Rum Lane and enquired if the mistress was at home. Having received an answer in the affirmative, Catherine alighted and was invited to come in. The owner of this house had formerly been one of Mrs Christy's confidential servants. With several others, she had received her freedom many years ago and, having saved a little money, and been helped a little occasionally by her kind mistress, she began as a cake bakery in Spanish Town and, ultimately, moved to Kingston where she had met with such success as enabled her to buy her son free and also to purchase the snug little house in which she then resided. Her cakes were now unrivalled by any in the city and, in fact, she could have spared a score of customers.

The letter from her old mistress, having been duly read and explained by her son, a lad of twenty, Catherine received a very hearty welcome and a sincere promise of co-operation in the business in hand.

After breakfast next morning, Catherine, her servant, and Mrs Fisher's son set out on a kind of voyage of discovery. They visited the poor house, the hospital and even the gaol and walked through innumerable streets and lanes but returned in the evening without having received any information of him whom they sought. The next day, they enquired at the eating house and at the hotels and taverns. They continued their perambulations and enquiries for a week without any success. At the expiration of [this time], Master Fisher began to fight rather shy and, in a few days more, pleaded some engagement and parted company. At the end of a fortnight, Diana, as Catherine's waiting woman was called, complained of 'stone bruise' and pain in the knees and went off on a kind of 'parole of honour' among her old friends who seemed to be rather numerous in and about the city.

For a day or two, Catherine remained quietly at home, closeted in a snug little room which answered not only for kitchen and hall, but as a repository for baked cakes, until called for by customers, with her new acquaintance, Mrs Fisher, who, having initiated two of her granddaughters into the mysteries of cake-making, and, what is of equal importance, cakebaking, never troubled her head about any culinary matter except her 'pepper pot'. This dish, so celebrated in the annals of creolism, the retailer of pastry maintained, never could be 'got up' properly without her special superintendence and, whenever the family were to enjoy this prime mess, the ingredients invariably passed through her careful hands and were minced, pounded, peppered and salted under her eyes.

Catherine Brown, having got into the good graces of her hostess, was entertained occasionally with an episode connected with her adventurous life.

Mrs Fisher was by birth an African. She had been stolen from her brother on the Guinea Coast by a kind of marauding party who carried her off and exchanged her and her two children for a keg of spirits and a couple of hatchets. By the captain who bought her, she had been brought, with a great many other Africans, to Jamaica and sold at auction, on the beach where they landed, in 'lots to suit purchasers'. She was bought by a planter who wanted active young women for field work. The lot to which she belonged consisted of twenty. Many of these, as well as herself, had children but, as the purchaser would not bargain for them, they were all sold to other persons. From the day of the sale to this hour, the old woman said, she had never seen or heard anything of these children. They were boys, one eight and the other ten years of age. She remained for fifteen years with her first master who used his slaves so cruelly, worked them so hard and fed them so badly that many of them died before he had settled his plantation. At his death, all the slaves were levied on for his debts and, again Mrs Fisher or, as she was called then, for she had never been baptized, Venus, was offered to the highest and best bidder. She now fell into the hands of a new master who resided in a town. He treated her kindly enough but his wife was a violent tempered woman and, under the influence of passion, would strike down her servants with the first missile that came to hand. On one occasion, she had knocked two of Venus' teeth down her throat with a large cellar key. She frequently sent them to the workhouse to be whipped and worked in chains, for a month at a time, for any trivial offences. Her mistress [having died] when she had lived with her five years, her master sold off his effects and, once more, Venus stood in the public mart. She now fell into the hands of Mr Christy who had, during his life time, used her, as well as his other slaves, very leniently. On his death, his widow gave all the slaves freedom and, as she had been her personal attendant, made her a present of £20 to 'begin the world with'. She soon after entered into the silken bands of matrimony and became Mrs Fisher and pastry-cook about the same time. Since that day, to use the old woman's own words, she had seen many 'up's and downs' and having at length buried her husband, she now lived, she thanked God, a very quiet, comfortable life. Soon after she had been sold to her first master, she had a child which died when eight years of age. So poignant was her grief on the death of this child that she made an attempt to hang herself. This having become known to her master, he had her confined for three months after every night in the bilboes. He also declared that, if she hung herself, she should be buried at a cross roads and a stake driven through her body. This threat, she said, had more effectually prevented her design than all the punishment she had endured. She also added that for twelve years after, she had regularly, year by year, offered an oblation of a fowl at the grave of her child.

The old woman also hobbled out on two occasions with Catherine, to enquire at places where she said it wasn't right for a young woman to go alone. On one of these occasions, to her great surprise and delight, she met with Mary Ann whose joy and astonishment at meeting with Catherine were unbounded. She embraced her affectionately and, after bestowing all the benedictions of the east, and thanking the Almighty for bringing her safely over the red sea, invited her home, and, what was better still, she gave information relative to Jackson since his arrival in town. He had called to see Mass George who, perceiving he was sick, asked him to stop a few days until he was better. He became worse and was confined to bed for three weeks during which time she had nursed him with great care and also made up for him a few articles of clothing which he had purchased since he came to Kingston. He had been forced to spend a great part of the money that had been reserved to pay his passage and appeared to have given up the idea of leaving the country until he had obtained some employment, and replenished his purse.

Nothing could be more opportune than the meeting between Catherine and Mary Ann. Not only had the former gained much useful information but had, now, an old friend as a companion who, for several reasons, was well qualified to assist her in the search after Jackson. As the reader might anticipate, these cronies had a great deal to communicate to each other that was interesting. Mary Ann had never felt any safety since the exposure and frustration of the plot on Wales. She said that she dreamed every night that she had been 'murdered and then drowned' in the river that ran so furiously near the estate and was always coaxing Mass George to go and live in one of the towns, the further from Wales the better. Whether Mary Ann's persuasions or a battle at single-stick which she had with the overseer conduced most to Waldy's renouncing his avocation as millwright for Tharp's estate in Trelawny, is a problem which we candidly declare ourselves incompetent to solve. Suffice it to say that Mass George had gone off 'without beat of drum' and entered into co-partnership with a millwright who was mending and making mills on a wholesale scale on the northside of the island. Although Kingston was the company's head-quarters, they put mills to right that had gone wrong all over the parish and, indeed, at times, so it was said, extended their operations even beyond its precincts. Mass George's station was at head-quarters but, owing to some of the journeymen in the pay of the firm having gone off rather clandestinely, on the score of being ground down in the matter of remunerations for work done and performed and considering the number of mills that would not go round, unless the wheelwrights went their rounds regularly to see after them, and how natural it must be for a party having so much to do with mills to be grinding, we are of the party that feel inclined to think it likely that the workmen's noses had been brought to the grindstone. Be this, though, as it may, Waldy, for the benefit of all concerned, was sent off to an estate at a distance of twenty miles to make such repairs as would suffice for 'the present distress' and thus, Mary Ann said she had nothing to do until his return but what she pleased. Consequently, she pleased to agree with Catherine for a promenade on the following morning when she hoped, through the information of Mr Feurtado, a druggist, with whom Jackson had become rather intimate, in consequence of his selling the strongest gingerbeer on Sunday evenings and cigars as medicine, to gain such information as might lead to his discovery.

TWELVE

*B*efore the receiving ship at Port Royal had fired her morning gun on the mound, Catherine and the dealer in dough were sipping their coffee in the little room that contained the huge chest in which was deposited the cakes that had been baked for her customers on the previous evening. The old woman, having decided on regaling the family with a pepper-pot dinner, as usual on these occasions, began her operations at an early hour. There was, as she said, a great deal to be done which her grand-daughters knew nothing about. Now as Mrs Fisher had invited Mary Ann before they parted the previous day, to come to see her on the morrow, there was a little pride in the business of the day. Besides, Catherine had hinted something about her Aunt Downy's knowledge of boiling pepper-pot that (to use not, perhaps, a very polite term) had 'stuck in the old woman's gizzard' and she was determined to bring her guest to confess that there was as much difference between Mary Downy's pepperpot and hers as there was between a greengage and a China orange.

On a large table which served for ironing, for Mrs Fisher was laundress as well as baker, stood part of the ingredients required for the mess. There were callaloo, kale, ockros, thyme, peppers, cocoas and plantains to make 'fuffoo' besides salt pork, white crabs and tripe. How these various articles were to be amalgamated we don't know, nor would the reader though we told him. Suffice to say, Mrs Fisher did.

Having cautioned Catherine to 'mine bring im fren to drink sum soop', she took a small key from her pocket and let her through the shop. She was 'fraid', she said, to open her gate as the work-house gang, with their chains and collars, were sweeping the streets before her house and they always begged her [for] bread … she paid taxes and was entitled to have [the street] before her house swept without giving away all her bread

... yes, she said, flour was very dear and wood was high and she had even to buy her water.

As Catherine passed out, she remembered that she had herself been in the house of bondage 'and looked at the rock from whence she had been hewn', [and] she gave the foremost of the chaingang a piece of silver to be divided among them and proceeded on her way. With Mary Ann she had breakfast and together they sailed forth to the ginger-beer fountain. They found the vendor of medicines at his post not engaged with prescriptions, as might have been expected, but opening a cask of American hams. In fact, although Mr Feurtado's sign intimated publicly that he was a 'Chemist and Druggist' and the large bottles of coloured water displayed in the windows, as well as the huge mortar and pestle painted in bright yellow on his sign-board corroborated the assertion, he dealt also in all kinds of groceries. And, although his religious creed prohibited his eating pork, he entertained no scruples about the sale of the article on the same principle that teetotalers retail grog.

The women passing under the yellow mortar entered the drug store and the man that sold hams and calomel, with all the politeness of a courtier, suspended his operations of unpacking the smoked provisions.

'Vat I can do for you, dish morning, ladies?' enquired Mr Feurtado, grinning and displaying a set of teeth sadly in want of a brush.

'We come, sar, fe ax if you please can tell me sa wa Mr Jackson top, sar,' replied Mary Ann.

'Me Gosh!' exclaimed the Israelite. ''Tis dat for you call me ways from me bishness? You think say me keep Missar Jackson in me pocket?'

'Hi, ole massa, you musn't bex. Dis lady come quite from Trelawny to look fe Mr Jackson,' said Mary Ann in a coaxing tone.

'Vell den. Missar Jackson board at the Red-Dragon. Now dere, you don't as bosher me na more bout Missar Jackson,' [he said]. And off went the druggist and chemist to his cask of hams and off marched Catherine and Mary Ann in search of the Red-Dragon. After asking a multitude of questions, they at length found the Red-Dragon, at an obscure boarding house for sailors in a very disreputable part of the city. After waiting in the yard of this place for a quarter of an hour, a miserable looking old seaman appeared with a white beard and red-cotton nightcap. He rubbed his eyes and looked dreamily at the women and, at length, being wide awake, gazed at them with a vacant stare. Without answering to their interrogatories, he exclaimed:

'Hello, Captain! There be two lassies below hatches axing after Jackson.'

'What kind of craft-square riggers?' enquired a voice from within, in a rather low tone.

'Reglar man-o-war cutters,' replied he of the red night-cap.

'Jackson went off to the Blue-Beard ten days ago. Ax the gals to come in,' said the invisible captain. The gals, however, declined the invitation and, more than half afraid, hurried off the premises and began enquiries about the Blue-Beard. Having been informed, however, of certain dangers which they would run by visiting this receptacle for discharged seamen, they prudently resolved on inviting the 'old lady' to accompany them to this place and, with this resolve, steered in the direction of Mrs Fisher's.

They found the old woman overlooking her grand-daughters who were performing sundry culinary operations in connection with cake baking and pepper-pot making.

Mrs Fisher dispatched her son to the Blue-Beard to make the necessary enquiries and entered into a kind of argumentative conversation with Mary Ann as to the *quantum sufficit* of 'meat' requisite to 'boil the pot' that bubbled before them. At length, after frequent tastings and pepperings, Mrs Fisher declared the mess to be fit for the table, and 'Sukey' was despatched for the old fashioned tureen that served, with other superannuated pieces of crockery, to ornament the sitting room. Catherine and Mary Ann preceded the soup into the house by twenty minutes and had time to crack half a dozen jokes at 'Mammy Fisher's' expense before dinner. The pepper-pot that had so much occupied Mrs Fisher's scullery was, by all, lauded to the skies and finally announced to be beyond all praise. The precocious juvenile that had been commissioned with enquiries to the Blue Beard now returned and reported 'non come-atable',[38] the doors and windows being barred, and by mutual agreement, further proceedings were postponed for the evening and a tour of discovery agreed on for the morrow by the triumvirate.

On Mary Ann's calling next morning, as per agreement, she found Catherine and her hostess sitting before a diminutive table that boasted only three legs. This tripedal article of household furniture was, like its owner, a sexagenarian. In its youthful days, its supporters had been quadruple, but having been subject to the gambols of a kid while bearing up a wedding cake that had been subjected to the sun's perpendicular rays and chimerical influence, it lost its equilibrium and one of its legs together.

As Mrs Fisher had promised to render her assistance in the further enquiries now to be instituted relative to the Blue Beard, she hastened to make preliminary arrangements in which the aid of both Sukey and Eliza were called into action and the Queen's English and Dr Syntax's head at once broken together, not for the first nor second time, by the following order, 'Lizar, bring I de tea caddy, let I locks it.' We are not, however, from this order to infer that Mrs Fisher meddled with Shoushong or Bohea. No, she was literally, in every sense of the word, a tea-totaller and ran as little risk of being killed by cannister as by grape. The fact was that 'tea caddy' and 'sugar trummel' were, in Mrs Fisher's vocabulary, synonymous terms and, as her granddaughters had a wonderful propensity to meddle with all kinds of saccharine matter, the locking process was only a conservative measure. Having given ample directions which, beginning with the sugar trummel, ended with the 'matches box', Mrs Fisher's locomotive powers were at length called into action. She, however, had occasion to return twice after starting in the first place to order the dog to be driven out of the kitchen and, in the second, to ascertain that the cat was not locked up in the pantry. She made an abortive attempt to return a third time, but at length bawled out to 'Lizar' to 'ten in de cake shop close' and got fairly under way.

As Mrs Fisher's topographical knowledge of Kingston was said (by herself) to be very great, she entertained sanguine hopes of being able, without any enquiries, to find her way to the Blue Beard. She discovered, however, that she had reckoned without her host, for several alterations on a rather extensive scale had been made in certain parts of the city since she had discontinued her peregrinations. An auxiliary being required, consequently, she bent her steps to Mrs Chataway's cake and blacksmith establishment in Cow-Hide lane. Mr Chataway shod horses and mended chaise springs and, his 'rib' made cakes and sold spruice-beer. The cakes were on a table, at the very threshold of the smithy door, covered with a white damask table cloth, the spruice-beer cooling in a tub of water under the table, and the forge and horses further in by a great deal. Mr Chataway stood by the anvil, hammer and drill in hand, and his wife sat in a very low chair making a pair of breeches for her son 'Charley'. Both of them were 'high coloured', one from the effects of soot and smoke and the other from being a quadroon.

Mrs Chataway, having expressed her surprise and satisfaction at seeing 'Mammy Fisher' whom she thought was dead (and no doubt hoped her cake shop was buried), presented her with the very low chair on which she had been sitting to make 'Mass Charley's' breeches and curtsied to her companions.

The old woman puffed and blew at a great rate and fanned herself with a blue cotton handkerchief. At length, having 'cooled down' she introduced her business, on which Mrs Chataway exclaimed:

'Hi, marm, you no bin yare say de Blue Bade gib up? Yes, marm, since after Chrismus, marm. Chatty,' she added, calling to her husband, 'can you tell say whey Mr Cumso move im tavern gone?'

'Cumso's house is done up … he failed last year. There's a Spaniard next door that keeps the Flying Dutchman, people say with the money Cumso robbed from his creditors. I dare to say the lady will find the gentleman she's enquiring for over there,' replied Mass Chatty who went on pointing his horseshoe nails.

The [search] party, after having some spruce-beer, started out in quest of the Flying Dutchman. From Mass Chatty's direction this task proved comparatively easy and a sign board, on which was painted a ship in full sail, soon informed them that they stood before the house in question. Señor Lopez was not at home but, having groped their way into the provision shop, they found two lazy-looking, overgrown lads in charge of that appendage to the Flying Dutchman. One of these promising boys, who answered to the name of 'Mucco Dick', desired the other, called Archy, to call Mr Lopez's 'lady' but, instead of obeying this mandate, Archy made a very cavalier reply and pouted his thick lips in such a way that Dick declared they looked just like 'a fippance salt pork'. This comparison Archy thought so odious that he instantly charged the aggressor with a yard stick with which he had been measuring some osnaburg for a fat maiden with little twinkling eyes and a very large mouth. Dick hurriedly snatched up the butter knife and stood on the defensive, on which Archy threw aside his weapon, doffed his Kilmarnock cap and tucked up his sleeves whereon Dick, placing himself in a pugnacious attitude, warded off a blow intended for his snout and, pitching head foremost into Archy, sent him heels over into the leaven trough that stood on the opposite side.

The fat girl, who had frequently before shown her teeth, now laughed very loudly, a privilege generally acceded to people with large mouths, [causing] Archy [to indulge] in some language at her expense which certainly was not as flowery as might have been expected from one who stood forth floured from head to foot. He, however, returned to the contest, on which 'Mucco Dick' stuck him against the wall, but finding perhaps that the paste contracted from the leaven tub was not sufficiently strong to hold him there, began to 'tack' him up when 'Mass Mick', the clerk, who was bottling porter below heard the hammering and, on coming up, was frightened to find Archy covered with leaven and consequently in a high state of fermentation, looking as wealy as an Irish potato and 'Mucco Dick' all tattered and torn. He swore that neither of the boys was worth a johnnycake, pronounced the scuffle a doughy affair and ordered the baker, 'Bandy John' to take them both to the workhouse to be whipped.

Senor Lopez's 'lady' who, must on the score of consistency, be [called] 'Señora', and who alone was conversant with lodging house affairs, now gave the party audience. She was a 'black-sambo', dressed in a white petticoat and yellow morning gown. Her head was tied with a flashy silk kerchief and she was slipshod and stockingless although gold, sufficient to purchase hose for [the rest of] her lifetime, glittered on various parts of her person. From the Señora they learned that Jackson had been connected with a fight which had taken place there the night before. She had not seen him since, for he had been wounded and taken to the Sailor's Home.[39] To this place she advised them to go. They easily found the place and Catherine and her companions were ushered into a room. As these rooms were separated by flimsy oznaburgh screens, all that was said in one could easily be distinctly heard in the other, and it required no attention to ascertain that oaths and curses were household words at the Sailor's Home. There seemed to be seamen of every grade, from the captain to his cook, assembled in this den and the smell of ardent spirits with the jingling of glasses clearly indicated that the inmates of the dingy eating room were making frequent attacks on the bottle.

'Where'd you heave to, to take aboard your breakfast, Jack?' enquired one of the motley crew.

'Came to anchor off the Dutchman in a gale last night, d'ye see Bill. Got a little topheavy at Patterson's groggery … couldn't bear up … so the d——d old Spaniard picked me up and make me pay for sleeping in the cook shop and for breakfast this morning,' replied Jack.

'There was the devil to pay there last night,' said Bill. 'Tom Pepper got his daylight darkened and his nose smashed as flat as a biscuit. He won't be on his pins this sometime. There was some bloody work done. The Spaniard says the d——d landowner had a 'bowie' in his sleeve.'

'The planter was wounded badly,' said one of the company. 'Besides, he is in limbo. Lopez swears he dived his knife into Señor Manuel as they call the old codger who was wounded. They say he's done up.'

'I want to keep dark about that there rumpus at the Dutchman,' said one of the men. 'Was the chap who was sent to the lock-up a skipper?'

'No, he was a kind of naygar driver like. He'd been on the "staff" this some time an' they bled him well nigh to his last quid o' bacco at the Blue-Beard.'

'Avast there, Tom,' said a sailor. 'Captain's agoin' to spin us a yarn.'

'Go ahead, we've all laid to,' replied Tom. 'Now Captain, one a them thoroughbred startlers, you know.'

The Captain then proceeded to give an account of some of his voyages which proved to be nearly as wonderful as those of Sindbad [sic].

'What straits did ye say, Captain?' enquired one of the party who was evidently half seas over.

'I've been up the Straits of Gibraltar and in the Straits of ...'

'I tell ye what it is Captain ...the only straits ye have been in were those near Cape Hard-up, when ye ran aground on the sea shore and couldn't find a bawbee in your breeches pocket. That was a devil of a strait ye were in last voyage. I know when old Sally lugged ye up afore the bench and ye couldn't fork out,' said the sailor that was half drunk. Here there was a roar of laughter and an awful clattering among the bottles and glasses.

'Tom's getting bushy,' said the Captain.

'Have yer ever been in Greece, Captain?' enquired someone.

'To be sure he has, messmate,' exclaimed Tom. 'The night he tumbled into the slushpot warn't he all over it, and be d——d to him.'

[Mrs. Fisher now applied to a little old woman who was crossing the room and the old woman went to the door and said, 'Missar Pintar] sumany wante peak wid you little'.

Mr Pintar made his appearance in the entry and, seeing females, shuffled his feet and bent his head as if he had some idea of making his obeisance. On Catherine's enquiry if Mr Jackson was, or had been a lodger at his houses he replied that 'a person of that name had been wounded in a scuffle at the Dutchman. He was brought to him bleeding from a wound in the head and he had put him to bed, but next morning Jackson had been arrested and taken to Gaol. He was pleased to add, however, that he had a man now in the house who could prove that Jackson was not in the room when the fight took place, but ran in, hearing the row, and was wounded by the Spaniard, and that he would, if the lady liked, go with her to the prison. This offer was readily accepted, and thither Catherine and Mary Ann, accompanied by the landlord of the Sailor's Home, directed their steps, while the old woman toddled home.[40]

After some demurring, the jailer permitted the party to enter the room where Jackson was confined. On a miserable pallet, languishing with fever, lay Jackson, so pale, emaciated and care-worn as to excite some doubts at first in the mind of Catherine as to whether or not he was the person they sought.

We will not here attempt to describe either Jackson's surprise or Catherine's mingled feelings of grief and joy. Mary Ann, too, shed [an] abundance of tears but wiped them soon and, by permission of the jailer (who seemed to think more highly of Mr Pintar than most persons did), went to get some clean water and soap to bathe the wound which, of itself, was not dangerous.

Catherine enquired if Jackson was bailable and was informed that he was not, as the man had died of his wounds. Catherine and Mary Ann remained until evening, when they left, their patient evidently somewhat better for their ministrations.

Though Catherine indulged in the most [poignant] grief as soon as she reached home, she could not but feel thankful that her exertions on Jackson's behalf had been, so far, crowned with success and she earnestly prayed that he might be rescued from the fearful charge now brought against him and from his present haunts and associates. From what she knew of his character, she entertained sanguine hopes of accomplishing the latter and, could she secure the sailor who said he could prove Jackson's innocence, as a witness, she thought the former at least feasible.

Mr Pintar had promised to interest himself on Jackson's behalf, whether from motives purely philanthropical or urged on by certain feelings of rivalry towards the master of the Flying Dutchman, who frequently inveigled boarders from the Sailor's Home, was purely problematical. Suffice it, however, to say he was unremitting in his exertions. He had the sailor, who was privy to the whole affair, examined on oath before the sitting magistrates and finally succeeded in turning the tables completely against Lopez. In order to effect this he, as well as Catherine and Mary Ann, had some hard battles to fight. The magistrates were reluctant to meddle in an affair they imagined to be beyond their jurisdiction and Lopez continued to frighten the sailor.

At length, it was determined to employ a lawyer, but there was only one independent enough to act against the Magistrates' veto, and he resided several miles from town. It having been thought that Catherine should proceed to this gentlemen's residence with the sailor's deposition, Mr Pintar's boy, Jacky, was sent to hire Mr Dove's pony and kittareen. As is well known, the negro is ever ready with nicknames and Mr Dove was better known by the rather rude cognomen of 'Nyam-to-hell' from his notoriety in handling the knife and fork. Jacky, who it would appear, had never been honoured with a personal introduction to the voracious Mr Dove, having arrived at that gentleman's beat, put forth the following query to a carpenter whose avocation had exalted him to the roof of same building:

'Massa can please tell me whey Missa Nyam-to-hell 'tap?'

'Yes, my boy,' replied the workman who happened to be the insulted Mr Dove himself, and who shingled houses as well as hired out equipages, 'wait until I come down and I'll show you.'

Dove, having reached *terra firma*, seized the unsuspecting Master Jacky and gave him such a belting that it was hard to tell whether he was a man or a monkey. The kittareen and pony were, nevertheless, sent to the order of Mr Pintar but, as the habiliments of the said Jacky had suffered so very seriously during the hiding he had recently undergone, and his wardrobe could offer no substitute, another promising lad connected with the establishment, called 'One-eye Cuffee', took his seat as coachman in the kittareen which bore some resemblance to a French diligence. It was supported by lofty wheels with loose tyres and hung on huge C springs. The shafts were straight, splintered and wound with bark rope, the paint had been rubbed off in some places and rose in blisters in others, while the lining hung in tatters. The pony was of the Lilliputian order, wall-eyed, bob-tailed, flap-eared, flea-bitten and scraggy in the extreme. His knees were broken and his hoofs split. His credentials, though, were of a high order and his master said he was a 'first-rate' pony and was better than he looked. He had been bred at the celebrated Shuttlewood Pen.

It was some time before he could be persuaded to go ahead but Jacky and a jolly tar, having shoved hard at the wheels, he at length started off at a spanking rate. 'One-eye Cuffee' drove the Shettlewood pony well. He had a tight rein, jerked the bit twice in three minutes and, stooping over the dash board, touched him on the fl ank with his short whip. The pony scampered down Duke Street, turned Pie-Corner (in doing which he overset an old woman's cake tray) and rattled the kittareen along, followed by several urchins screaming at the top of their voices, 'Cuffee, tek de shine out a him! Tek de shine out a him!'

Catherine's interview with the retired lawyer was highly satisfactory and resulted in the apprehension and imprisonment of Lopez and in Jackson being admitted to bail. He was then removed from the prison to Waldy's and, very soon, [he] recovered his health. The trial took place at the Grand Court which followed when the Spaniard was found guilty of manslaughter and Jackson fully acquitted on the clearest evidence.

A few days after the trial of Jackson, Catherine was agreeably surprised to meet with her old friend Vernon in Kingston. He had landed only a few days before. There was a little romance, at once pleasing and interesting, in his return to the island. Our readers will remember the commission with which Vernon had been entrusted by Mr Fleming, relative to his wife's sister. In consequence of the demise of his father, other matters had so entirely engrossed his mind and occupied his time, that no enquiries had been instituted at that time.

After Celeste sailed with Mrs Christy, Vernon took up the miniature of her mother and the striking likeness which it bore to her greatly enhanced it in his estimation, though this was a secret locked in the recesses of his heart. Just then, his mother entered his chamber and desired in a playful way to be favoured with a sight of the angel by whom he had been smitten. He complied, but before he could explain, Mrs Vernon exclaimed:

'Gracious Heavens! My boy, how came this miniature into your possession? It is the likeness of my sister Sophia,' and, touching a secret spring, she opened the locket and displayed her name, the date of her birth and a lock of her hair.

The documents received with the miniature, together with the narrative related by Mr Fleming, removed every shadow of doubt from the mind of Vernon that in his mother he beheld Charlotte, the aunt of Celeste.

A kind of mutual explanation here followed. Mrs Vernon excused herself for not having acquainted her son with any of the circumstances of her early life on the score of an injunction laid on her by his father, while the son informed his mother of his passion for Celeste. It was for the purpose of soliciting her hand that he had returned to the island.

As for Jackson, he had been taught a lesson and, if he had paid dearly for his indiscretions, he had only done that which thousands had done before. Through the interest of Mrs Christy, he obtained a situation as wharfinger and, with her approbation, married Catherine shortly after. Their son, having received a tolerable education, returned to the country, was brought up by Waldy as a millwright and became a very reputable tradesman.

Mr Vernon won the heart and gained the hand of his handsome cousin, much to the satisfaction of her father and, shortly after, they returned to England.

Mrs Christy died at the age of seventy-two. She bequeathed the principal part of her fortune to charitable institutions but left Mrs Vernon, junior, two thousand pounds and Catherine five hundred. On each of her servants, she bequeathed thirty pounds. As for Mary Ann, she still resides in Kingston with 'Mass George' but whether as his wife or mistress we are unable to state, having lost sight of them for several years past.

Catherine became an excellent woman. She read many hours a day and, at length, could converse with a degree of elegance, though she always retained her shy and retiring habits and, to her credit be it said, on receiving the legacy from Mrs Christy, she immediately tendered two hundred pounds as payment for her freedom to the proprietor of Greenside. But he returned it with a kind letter from old Mr Cunningham who had heard of her adventurous life from the attorney and likewise from Mr Vernon whom he had met in England ... and Catherine was heard to say frequently that to know her old master forgave her afforded her more heartfelt satisfaction than the receipt of Mrs Christy's legacy.[41]

THE END

Endnotes

1   In the original manuscript, this chapter was given the title 'Busha's Mistress'.

2   This word 'tabour' is not in the original document but was an editorial note in the published newspaper version.

3   At this point, a section of the manuscript is deleted and the story picks up at 'The climate...'

4   In the manuscript version, it is difficult to decipher this word, but 'crop house' seems more appropriate.

5   In the original manuscript, chapter 2 does not begin here and hence does not have a title. The decision to make this a separate chapter appears to have been made by Miss L.G. Perkins. See 4/26/6, fol. 19.

6   This paragraph was omitted in the later version.

7   Most of this paragraph was omitted in L.G. Perkins' typescript.

8   The manuscript is unclear at this point. The sentence beginning 'Then turning to Jackson he continued . . .' was a construction by the editors of the *Daily Telegraph and Jamaica Guardian* and retained by Miss Perkins.

9   Someone inserted the word 'water' here.

10   A sentence is missing at this point, as the manuscript is torn.

11   In Miss Perkins' version, the text reads 'who is that pretty girl who lives with Mrs Christy', but this is an unlikely reading and the manuscript is torn at this point.

12   The manuscript is torn here, so a filler has been added.

13   This 'house' was called a 'negro cottage' during the slavery era.

14   An alternative title, or, perhaps a subtitle, 'Quammin, the Dungeon and the Duppy', appears to have been added; see f. 18 of 4/26/6.

15   Spelt 'Quammin' in the original manuscript, but this is the more usual spelling.

16   We are unsure if this is 'leg-bail' or 'leg-ball'.

17   At this point, folios 55–73 are missing from the original manuscript. In the newspaper version, the editors wrote: 'Parts of the original MSS. are here unreadable owing to the ravage of time and worms. We have taken the liberty of substituting a paragraph to give the story a connected form at this spot.' The newly constructed parts are from 'The excitement' to 'side board'. Folio 74 begins, 'As the decanter...'

18   In the original manuscript, there is no chapter designated '4', and hence this division appears to have been an editorial decision, beginning chapter 4 at f. 79.

19   '...on her household management' does not appear in the original manuscript. Instead, there is a word that looks like 'reconnomics'. See f. 79.

20   The end of this sentence is an addition by the newspaper editors and is not in the original manuscript. The sentence in the manuscript is hard to decipher and runs something like 'In the gross . . . human nature acknowledges . . . it is intuitively given to . . . with the oppressed'.

21 Words are missing here.

22 Folio 117 ends here and folios 118–121 are missing. From 'The individual' to 'harbour' has been inserted by the newspaper editors.

23 These two last sentences were crossed out in the original but inserted by the newspaper editors.

24 This chapter was entitled 'The Attorney's Story' in the original manuscript (fol. 130).

25 This appears to be an error. Although the writing is unclear at this point, the word looks rather like 'fortune' or 'future'. See fol. 130.

26 This last part of the sentence does not appear in any of the other versions. See fol. 130.

27 For some reason, the newspaper editors or Miss Perkins substituted 'wild' for the author's original word 'lascivious'.

28 A note in the original text reads: 'Under the Slave Code of Jamaica obeah was a capital offence. Such was the lamentable effect produced by this superstition on the negro mind that hundreds have been known to sink beneath its influence in the course of a single year. Having once become persuaded that they were under the influence of this spell their spirits forsook them, life lost all its charms, the body became emaciated, and no effort could save the victim from an untimely grave.'

29 Miss Perkins's typescript has a note at this point which reads: 'Several pages of the M.S.S. are here missing, covering the end of chapter 7 and the beginning of chapter 8, which evidently dealt with a raid by the militia on a group of runaway slaves, who were aided by the maroons.' The newspaper edition reads: 'Several pages of the manuscript are here missing. They evidently deal with the Maroon Uprising which must be familiar to the student of Jamaican history. The news of the uprising sent a party of Englishmen from around Greenside to go and meet the rebel band which was operating in the vicinity.' However, there is no indication from the original manuscript either that chapter 7 ended at this point, or that any folios are missing. It is true that a page seems to have been cut out, but there is no gap in the numbering sequence of the folios. The author may simply have cut out the page and continued his writing.

30 This does not appear to be in the original manuscript, which is difficult to decipher but reads something like 'Then their mothers . . .'

31 A line is missing in the manuscript which is faded. Neither of the previous versions managed to decipher it. The faded line starts (after 'liard'), 'Be this as it may' and ends with 'appears'.

32 The manuscript is indecipherable at this point and a sentence is left out. See f. 173.

33 The manuscript is unclear at this point and a few words have to be left out.

34 The manuscript is smeared at this point (f. 175) and is indecipherable.

35 Quite a few lines have been left out at this point owing to the poor state of the manuscript. See. fol. 176.

36 The manuscript is unclear at this point, and newspaper editors inserted 'conquered him' as a construction.

37 From 'As soon as' to this point is quite damaged in the original manuscript (ff.181– 182); so much of this is constructed.

38 Seems more like 'non-comestible'.

39 A folio is missing at this point.

40 The top left hand corners of folios 236–247 are damaged so that all versions have constructed text at points in this chapter.

41 This is not the original ending of the novel, but folio 247, the last folio, is unreadable, and the newspaper editors and Miss L.G. Perkins ended the novel here.

APPENDIX I

The Poetry of Cyrus Francis Perkins

Donald McDonald

The Scottish Overseer.

My Busha was a Highland
The scion of a famous clan,
As bonny and braw a lad
As ever wore the Scottish plaid.

In days of feuds – tradition said
His sires had oft for freedom bled,
And still they were a martial race
And leved and gloried in the chase.

Our here too could hunt the stag
From morn till night, from crag to crag,
And may a day, mid brush and brake
He'd stop to eat his barley-cake.

At length gaunt famine reached his cot
And peeped into the porridge pot,
Both kith and kin were sorely tried
The grain grew scarce, the cattle died.

And oft as Fortune's wheel went round
The fickle jade upon them frowned;
So Donald though to win her smile
In this far distant sunny isle.

For he had heard the golden tide
Ran in the West both deep and wide.
So, once resolved, he made the trip
And landed from a Glasgow ship.

And here he met with quite a botch
Of English, Irish, and of Scotch.
Fish from Shannon, Thames, and Tweed
And others too of mongrel breed.

For in this tropic isle there grows
The shamrock, thistle and the rose,
All these had left their native fold
And wandered forth in quest of gold.

Their coffers filled would cross the seas
Regain their homes, and live at ease.
And thus it was, Jamaica's spoil
Served to enrich some other soil.

But hie we to our Celtic friend
Whose fortunes soon began to mend.
A little past his second year
He gained the rank of overseer.
This, some book-keepers well may grudge
Who had, for seven years, to trudge.
Alas he had grim death to thank
For gaining soon as high a rank.

This Busha, how, no one could tell
Stumbled one dark night down the well.
A jury sat, and tus they struck it –
'Fell down the well and kicked the bucket.'

Poor man, he died without confessing
Left Mack his shoe-horn and his blessing,
But what, perhaps, was better worth
His snug and comfortable berth.

He had the horn, so Trustees choose
To let him heel on Sandy's shoes.
What though they were a little large
The attorney came and gave him charge.

Rode up and down and through the lanes
Round the fields and saw the canes,

Viewed the cattle, carts and wains
Counted out the cattle chains.

Then to the Great House he did ride
The new fledged Busha at this side,
Here, they books and papers signed
And then of course, the party dined.

In those days Busha's all lived well
As many a turkey's ghost could tell.
Supplies were yearly sent him out -
A cask or two of good brown stout.

Beef, pork, butter, rice, split peas
A hamper too of Gloster cheese.
Twice per week his boy would call
For fresh beef at the butcher's stall.

And a slave who was employed to fish
Each day supplied a famous dish,
Of mullets, conchs, and lobsters too
Of which he made a savory stew.

Watchmen now and then would bring
Shrimps and crawfish from the spring,
And in their season, without fail
Ducks, baldpate, and fat ringtail.

Of pigs has numbered seven score
Twixt China sow and mountain boar,
And, not to mention other stock
The poultry yard showed quite a flock.
Besides each overseer would keep
For his own use, a flock of sheep;
And, as they had abundant feed
They well might view with Southdown breed.

But Busha would have thought it pelf
To keep these good things to himself
His house was open as his heart
The humblest stranger shared a part.

154

And his larder's very best
Was freely offered to his guest.
Indeed to prove his welcome true
He often made his guest quite 'fou.'

The stranger's room was always kept
For where one dined, of course he slept.
On festive days some were just able
To stretch himself beneath the table.

If squeamish next day, then mayhap
Each one would take a 'leetle drap,'
Of milk, quite fresh, just from 'the bull'
Maybe, perhaps, a thimble full.

Because twas said 'hair from the hound
Would very often heal the wound'.
Still Donald's heart was ill at rest
The love of home burnt in his breast.

His broad claymore hung o'er his bed
To mind him of old times, he said;
For often when he wore the kilt
This weapon dangled at his belt.

The sword had served full many turns
Some said it once belonged to Burns.
While others thought that it had not
But was the gift of Walter Scott.

But he could stronger proof adduce
T'was worn by Wallace and by Bruce,
And it was worth each Scotian's while
To kiss its trusty blade and smile.

Yes! Well he loved dear Scotia's shore
And longed to see its hills once more.
And often in his midnight dreams
He'd wander by the mountain streams.

And then he'd fancy that he could
See the 'brown heath and shaggy wood',
He'd dream oft too of Jess McCrone
And what a buxom lass she'd grown.

Before him stood the blushing maid
With cheeks as ruddy as her plaid,
Till he returned, she vowed she would
Never lay aside the silken snood.

In dreams men oft take rapid flight
His Highland glen was soon in sight.
He saw the hawthorn in the dell
The thistle and the sweet blue bell.

His native cot, the old grist mill
Were standing as he left them, still.
And as he onward urged his way
He heard the well-known bark of Tray.

The queen of night was on her wane
He reached the door, looked through the pane,
He saw the cheerful supper spread
Sweet buttermilk and barley bread.

The gude wife and his sire were there
Content made sweet their humble fare.
The big 'Ha Bible' claimed their care
And then came forth the evening prayer.

The light was streaming through the thatch
He raised his hand and reached the latch.
He pulled – his claymore tumbled down
And nearly broke his hapless crown.

For as you, just above, have read
His sword and belt hung o'er his bed.

A Fragment

[First part missing]

...And terror sits throned in each lordly face,
A hand appears, and the fingers write –
O'er where the candlestick throws its light.
The monarch's heart it troubled now,
And fear is stamped on his royal brow,
The guests are mute the music ceased
And the seers are called to the royal feast.
But the writing that with such luster shone
Was the work of a Scribe, to them, unknown.
They tremble and gaze in wild dismay,
With nerves unstrung they turn away.
Then quickly they call the Hebrew sage
Who reads and explains the Scared Page.
'Thy reign, Oh! King – shall shortly end
Jehovah, thou hast dared offend
Thy gods have praised, and him defied,
Who only should be glorified.
And thou, Oh King! Of Claldee crowned
By him art weighed, and wanting found.'

On that night was Belshazzar slain
And Darius, the Mede, began to reign.

The Planter's Petition[1]

Oh! Hear a suffering planter's cry, who groans against Free Trade
    And do believe him when he says, no sugar can be made
Because the slender means he had, have all been risked and lost.
His last year's crop, in bond, did not pay more than its first cost
For he has tried with might and main to keep out of the mire,
    And now he hardly can pay up his stoker at the fire.
Sheep, hogs and poultry used to form a part, once, of his stock
    His farmyard now can only boast a single turkey cock,
    And he doth gobble all day long, at least so it is said
Against the British Government, cheap sugar and Free Trade.
    When formerly he rode abroad a charger was his pride,
    But now a meager pony or a mule he has to ride
And then so homely in his garb, so meanly he's equipped
That everybody plainly sees poor Busha's wings are clipped
His elbows both are sticking out, quite broken through the stitches;
    He hardly has a button left on any of his breeches.
His pasture walls are lying low, quite level with the ground
    And often are his meagre stock taken from out the pound.
Oh Downing Street! Oh cruel grey! Oh listen to his cries
    And do not still persist to say, 'The croaking fellow lies.'
Our dear, good-natured old Jon Bull, our isle to ruin goes
Because you suffer knaves and fools lead you to the nose.
Oh Daughters of Old England, I wish that you could see
    The human gore you swallow down in every cup of tea.
    The treaties signed long time ago are lying in the shade
While Spain and Brazil daringly still carry on their trade,
The bones of murdered millions are bleaching in the sun
While still the coffin slave ship her fateful course doth run.

Contentment and Principle

Whilst others that surround me pine because they have not more
Content, I can, with cheerful heart, enjoy my humble store,
My neighbours' sumptuous fare ne'er grudge, his dainties envy not
Nor murmur at the wise decree that fixed my humble lot.

His mansion with its wide domain, abundant store afford
My cottage ground supplies my wants for frugal is my board;
I see the wealthy pass me by, the scornful and the proud
Who hardly deign to notice me, an atom in the crowd.

Still, fairly launched on life's broad stage, I'll boldly play my part
And follow on where duty leads, with fixed and steadfast heart,
By chart and compass shape my course, nor would I madly dream
Whilst yet the cateract's roar I hear to trust the treach'rous stream.

I am not high, nor meanly stoop, but choose the golden mean
Disdain not aid, yet care not much on friendship's arm to lean,
I fear no foe, yet ever strive to give offence to none
Nor would I crush the meanest worm that crawls beneath the sun.

I have no wish that others should their compass square with mine
And take good heed none gauge me with another's plumb and line;
I would not venture in the storm, 'cause others risk the gale
But whilst the tempest rages high, with prudence furl my sail.

Why may I not my anchor cast and calmly ride at ease
And leave the headstrong crew who will to sail the boisterous seas?
Yes, I can sit secure and smile upon the peaceful shore
Regardless of the motley throng that struggle at the oar.

Contentment, heaven's great boon I claim, this soothes my heart to rest
Sweet solace of my pilgrimage, I clasp thee to my breast
Without thy aid, vain man would still in hapless misery pine
Though he could grasp the priceless wealth of dark Golconda's mine.

Or could he yet by occult art stern nature's laws unfold
And find the stone whose potent touch could turn his trash to gold,
Would that the blind and giddy throng that climb ambition's hill
Were brought to feel what e'er they grasp is but a shadow still!

That when the climax they have reached, with strife and care and pain
And grasped the prize, they will be called to lay it down again,
And in exchange, be forced to take, all that this world e'er gave
A troubled spirit, broken heart, a coffin and a grave.

Bonny Jean[2]

My lassie is both blithe and fair
No flower with her would dare compare,
The rose upon its thorny tree
Is not by half so sweet as she.

The bright black eye that beams on me
Fills oft my soul with joy and glee,
Let others choose as beast they see
Bonny Jean's the lass for me.

Her heart is loving, kind and true
Her grace and mein are matched by few;
Then while my heart and hand are free
My bonny Jean's the lass for me.

Should fortune frown and cast my lot
On some bleak shore or lonely spot,
Be it o'er the mountain, o'er the sea
Bonny Jean's the lass for me.

Visit To My Wife's Grave in the Old Churchyard Falmouth 1849[3]

Many years have past by, and the ivy grown high
  Since they sacred portals I trod,
  Thou art sacred to me, and ever must be
  For my kindred lie under thy sod.

Thy old Sabbath bell, it sounds I know well
  For oft hath it called me to pray.
  There, in days of my youth, I heard the great truth
  That Christ was the life and the way.

Now I visit a grave where tall cypresses wave
  Marked by an old willow tree;
  There, beneath the cold stone, a heart once my own
  From sighing and sorrow lies free.

Why, hardly can tell, as if bound by a spell
  I linger at this solemn spot;
  While time seems to fly, as rapidly by
  As if the dove's wings he had got.

And oh! Tell me not, whilst I kneel at this spot
  'The slumbering dead ne'er awake,'
  For the righteous shall rise, and ascend to the skies
  Of glory and bliss to partake.

And, 'Father' I said, as the broken heart bled
  And the gushing tears rolled on my cheek,
  'Thy hand struck the blow, that laid my hopes low
  Oh! Make me submissive and meek.'

Adieu! Sacred pile, we must part for awhile
But I trow we shall soon meet again,
For my frame is but dust and I feel that it must
In the dark, silent tomb soon be laid –

When in glory we meet, our crowns at the feet
Of Him who has loved us, we'll cast,
And, united, we'll raise the new song of praise
That shall through eternity last.

The Bottle

What caused me through the street to reel
And robbed me of my cheerful meal
And urged me on to cheat and steal
    The Bottle.

What stripped from off my back, the coat
Continues still my face to bloat,
But that on which all drunkards doat
    The Bottle.

What caused my friend to turn his back
And always to avoid my track,
And whistle me out in a smack?
    The Bottle.

What raised the blush upon the cheek
Of yonder woman mild and meek
And forced her, charity, to seek?
    The Bottle.

What filled the world with tears and groans
And strewed it o'er with human bones?
The drunkard answers, as he moans
    The Bottle.

What hastened Babylon's last fall
Provoked the writing on the wall?
And spread death through the banquet hall?
    The Bottle.

What put the crew all 'hard alee'
And caused the vessels loss at sea.
It was, the shipwrecked all agree
The Bottle.

What caused me with kind friends to part
And broke my aged parents' heart,
And said to happiness depart?
The Bottle.

The Deep Blue Sea[4]

The deep blue sea, the deep blue sea
There's music in its roar for me
I love its billows rolling high
I love the ocean's azure sky.

Oh! Tell me not of moonlit lake
Where lovers of true bliss partake
Of ruined castles, pointing high
Their mould'ring turrets to the sky.

For had I smiling parks ashore
And mountains of the yellow ore,
They'd bring but little joy to me
Could I not yet traverse the sea.

I envy not the tilted dame
Who glories in her rank and fame;
To neither knight nor lord I'd crouch
To gain his hand or silken couch.

Rocked by the billows on the deep
I tranquil lie and calmly sleep,
Contented that my humble lot
Is with the sailor in his cot.

Whilst life shall last, the deep blue sea
My loved, my cherished home shall be,
And when I die, oh! Let my grave
Be beneath the mountain wave.
The wild wind as it whistles by
Shall chant for more an anthem high,
And the wild and dashing surge
Shall raise for me a funeral dirge.

The Coolie's Grave

T'was where the tranquil waters of
The Rio Cobre glide,
The Coolie, now worn by disease
Had stretched himself and died.

Beneath the cumbrous cotton tree
That lent its friendly shade –
Now feeling that his and drew nigh
His humble couch he made.

False and visionary schemes
Had lured him from his cot,
And now, far from his native hills
He mourned his wretched lot.

No human hand is near to smooth
The lair on which he lies;
No friendly aid to soothe his mind
Or close his dying eyes.

Through the long watches of the night
In some uneasy dream,
His fancy brought to mind once more
The Ganges' sacred stream.

He raised his now dim eye to heaven
And cried, 'Oh! Bramah hear!
And then he offered to his God
His short and humble prayer.

'Ganges – Ganges' murmured he
Once more on Bramah cried,
Once more he raised his eyes to heaven
And then the Coolie died.

Just on the margin of the stream
Where graceful bamboos wave,
Some strangers, as they passed along
Had dug his narrow grave.

The traveler, as he journeys on
May see the hillock rise;
Beneath – his wrapper for a shroud
The Asiatic lies.

Columbia[5]

Hark! The cannon's deadly roar
Pealing on Columbia's shore –
To arms! To arms! The cry is rife;
And now begins the mortal strife
And kindred blood must dye the sod
On which the Pilgrim Fathers trod.

The friends, who late with jovial song
Oft would the midnight hour prolong,
Now meet like demons in the fight
With bitter hate and deadly spite
And kindred blood must dye the sod
On which the Pilgrim Fathers trod.

A brother's hand now strikes the blow
His dagger lays a kinsman low;
Perchance, tis buried in that breast
On which his aching head found rest,
And kinsman's blood must dye the sod
On which the Pilgrim Fathers trod.

Those whom the same lov'd land gave birth
Yea, those who gathered round one hearth,
And in sweet bonds of sympathy
Around one altar bent the knee
Now spill their blood and dye the sod
On which the Pilgrim Fathers trod.

A tear may well dim every eye
And every bosom heave a sigh,
When sire and son to passion yield
And cross their sabers on the fi eld
And dye with kindred blood the sod
On which the Pilgrim Fathers trod.

Who tells where feuds like these will end
What these gigantic schemes portend?
Ah! Who shall count the widow's sighs
Or mark the hapless orphan's cries
For kindred blood that dies the sod
On which the Pilgrim Fathers trod.

The stripes torn from Columbia's flag
Will leave a blood stained, tattered rag,
Yet if her stars that remnant bear
She may rise glorious, free and fair
No bondsman's blood shall dye the sod
On which the Pilgrim Fathers trod.

Endnotes

1   Note by Lilly Perkins: 'The balance of the poem is destroyed'.
2   Written to his first wife, Jane O'Sullivan of Cork, Ireland who was buried in the old Falmouth churchyard.
3   Several members of the family were buried in Falmouth churchyard, including the author's father, who was a doctor to the regiment stationed at that town. An extension of the present church was built over some of the graves.
4   Note by Lilly Perkins: 'Written at the request of the Captain's wife, with whom the author returned to Jamaica in 1848, and who had traversed the ocean with her husband ever since their union sixteen years before'.
5   Written at the commencement of the American Civil War.

APPENDIX II
Genealogy of Perkins Family

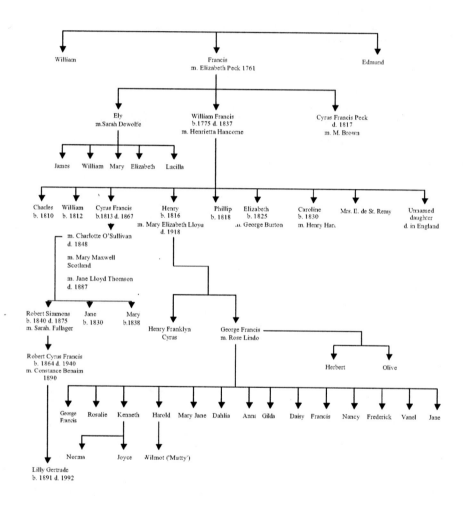

University of the West Indies, Mona, Jamaica, and The University of Hull, UK, from data in the Island Record Office (IRO), Twickenham Park, St. Catherine, Jamaica, as well as information supplied by Lilly, Norma and Joyce Perkins. See IRO, Trelawny Copy Register of Baptisms, Marriages and Burials, Vol. 1, 1770-1839, Perkins Gifts and Deposits, Jamaica Archives, 4/26, and F. Douglas Reville, *History of the County of Brant* (Bransourcetford, Ontario: The Hurley Printing Company, 1920), Vol. 1, p. 88. Constructed by Ahmed N. Reid.

APPENDIX III

Some of the Enslaved People on Greenside Estate, 1817

Source: 'Slave Registration and Compensation Records,' Public Record Office, T.71

Printed in the United States
32829LVS00003B/88-510

9 789766 370442